Breaking Free

Robyn Lindsey

Cover design DragonBone Designs

Portland, Oregon

Tri Oak Publishing

Oregon City, Oregon

© 2014

ISBN-13:
978-0989541640 (Tri Oak Publishing)

ISBN-10:
0989541649

Dedication

This book is dedicated to my mother, Barbara Nell Meeks. Her struggles were great, her life was much too short. In the end, she chose what was best for her children.

Acknowledgments

This book would never have been completed without the unending support of my love, Aaron. Also on my side cheering me on were my sons, my best friend Christine, Karla, Theresa, Teresa, Eileen, and so many others. My reader along the way, who is also in the book: Cathy... to you I say thank you so much! You are all so important to me.

The cover artwork is the work of Erin at DragonBone Designs in Portland, Oregon. www.dragonbonedesigns.com .

Chapter 1

Sam could tell that something was amiss as soon as she arrived at Redwood Landing, the assisted living facility that she worked at as a medication aide. There was nothing out of place, no noticeable smells, but there was an odd sort of hush and a lack of movement. Normally this time of day there were a few staff members moving from room to room, and at least one readying the dining room for breakfast which was now only a couple hours away. Sam knew something was going on so she went straight to her boss' office.

Samantha's boss, Jack, was one of the kindest men that she knew. He had a way of seeing what she was capable of before she even had a clue. When Jack saw that Sam was good at something, he made sure to utilize her for that task as much as possible. One of Samantha's strengths, as Jack noticed, was handling all of the details when a resident had passed away. Sam was very calm and respectful when dealing with the residents at all times but seemed to be extremely comforting to family members when there was a death.

"I need you to go up to Bill's room. He's gone. You know what to do, and I wanted you to be the one to handle everything," Jack told her.

Samantha simply nodded and exited his office. She was saddened to know that Bill was gone and didn't want Jack to see her emotion. Sam took a deep breath and walked up the stairs, she felt as if there was lead in her feet. It seemed like she was moving in slow motion to Bill's second story room.

Her heart hurt, Bill was one of her favorites. Bill always reminded Sam of an old sailor, with a scruffy beard and a pipe. He was a salty old man, always flirting, and never worrying about what might be "politically correct." He always told her that he was much too old to worry about such things. Bill had always had a joke, and they were often quite off-color. Sam had seen him make many of the young staff members blush, and Bill had often told her that what he liked about her is that she could dish it right back to him. Samantha made a point of remembering jokes to tell him. In fact, she had come in just this morning prepared to tell him a joke about a bow legged deer walking out of the woods. She knew that Bill would slap his knee and laugh with that twinkle in his eyes.

She paused, almost imperceptibly, before opening the door to Bill's room. He was still sitting on his couch, with his pipe in his lap. Sam was surprised by how peaceful Bill looked, both peaceful and a bit mischievous, that's how she would describe him in this moment. His lips were upturned at the sides, and it appeared he was smiling, as if he saw something that made him very happy right at the end. His leathery skin had permanent laugh lines around his eyes, his smile was etched in the corners of his mouth.

An aide had found him unresponsive in his room, the nurse pronounced him dead, but Jack had asked that anything else wait. Everything froze in time until Sam arrived. And now, she directed, and everyone moved around the room. They put fresh sheets on the bed, and made sure that everything in the room was tidy. Bill was carried to the bed and Sam washed his face, touching his cheek after she did so.

Sam bent down and kissed Bill's cheek after the aides had left the room, "I will miss you, Bill" she whispered as a tear rolled down her face. She allowed herself a moment, then Samantha quickly composed herself and called Bill's family. She sat with Bill while she waited for them, alternating between holding Bill's hand and tidying the room. She wanted things to be nice when his family got there, yet she wasn't quite ready to let go of her friend's hand. When they arrived, Sam sat with them, she handed them tissues and assured them that he went peacefully, in the night, while cleaning his pipe. Sam didn't leave the room until the funeral home had collected the body and the family had left.

"I'm going on a break, Jack," Sam said as she walked into his office.

"Are you alright?" Jack asked, looking into her eyes.

"I'm ok, but I will miss Bill. And this is 13. Thirteen deaths that I have personally handled. I think it's time for others to catch up," she said.

"I understand, Sam, but the way you handle everything... with such grace and respect. This is what you are meant to do," Jack said, and he watched Sam leave the room quietly. He knew that it put a strain on Samantha each time she had to handle a death, but she made it look so effortless and seemed to bounce back quickly. He made a mental note to check in with her later.

Sam walked through the kitchen, out the back door and sat down outside the kitchen door. It was often a vacant spot, unless Russ, the cook, was out smoking, but it was during breakfast now so Samantha knew she would have some alone time. She wanted to think about life, about what it all means, about whether Bill had any regrets. Then her cell phone beeped. It was a text from John, reminding her of their meeting later.

Sam and John had been married for 6 years. And they were now meeting to divide their property. Sam didn't want to go to the meeting. They had been divorced for just a few months and she would never let him know how much she missed him. She was so tired. Samantha just wanted John to be free and happy, and to move on with his life.

When Samantha walked back in, she grabbed a plate of food that Russ had set aside for her. Today was pancakes and sausage links. She grabbed the syrup bottle and poured a small amount onto her pancake stack. He always had a plate ready for her it seemed. Sam went into the break room where she hoped to eat. Instead, she walked in on hushed whispers.

"She's so cold," one of her coworkers said.

"I know, she acts like death is nothing, it's like it is just business to her," another replied.

It wasn't the first time that Sam had caught them talking behind her back, and she quickly exited. She stood in the kitchen, eating a few bites and tossing the rest in the garbage. Sam had no time to dwell now, though, as her break time was over and she had work to do. The residents of the assisted living were finishing their breakfast in the dining room and Sam went from table to table, quietly letting them know that their friend Bill had passed. She held their hands, shared in their sadness, and mourned a friend with them. Sam had tissues, but her eyes remained dry. Samantha had shed her tears in private. Her job now was to remain strong and support them.

The rest of the shift was spent playing catch up from the morning. Sam was thankful for the hustle and bustle, she was thankful for not having the time to think about all the twists and turns of life, and of death. Thinking about death always made Samantha ponder each loss she has experienced, but she quickly pushed those thoughts out of her mind. Almost too quickly, her shift was over and it was time for her appointment with John.

The drive to the cafe was shorter than she would have liked, she had not been looking forward to this meeting, and it had already been a rough day. Samantha was a few minutes early and sat at a table while she waited. Out of habit, she ordered black coffee for John, while she began drinking her mocha. He was right on time, and leaned across the table to kiss her on the cheek.

"So how are you, Sam?" John asked.

"I'm ok. Very tired. Bill passed away last night," she responded

John offered his condolences and instinctively reached across the table to caress her hand. His hand almost made it to hers, but he quickly drew it back. "Sorry, habit," he said, "so we need to decide what you want to keep and what I keep."

Sam felt the tears rising as he pulled away from her, but she fought them back. She refused to show weakness, as always. Samantha was left feeling like she always did, she wished that she could open up to him but had no idea how. If she could, she would reach across the table and grab his hand, or move next to him and put her arm around him and hold him tight. Yet she stayed where she was.

"I have everything I need," Sam told him, "I don't have a lot of extra room, and I have what I need."

"Alright, I understand that," John said "but I can't take everything. How about if we have a yard sale to get rid of all the extra and split the money?"

Chapter 2

The drive back to her small apartment made her feel lonely. The boxes, the very few things she had, were all unpacked and everything was put in it's proper place. She had nothing to clean, nothing to put away. Sam did not like to be idle, and even pondered messing things up just so she would have things to do but realized that would be futile.

A walk would be good, she thought, so out she went. Sam had not explored much in her new neighborhood. She walked out of her apartment, and out to the road. She noticed license plates from at least six different states, she saw several cats in windows, and some flower boxes that were blooming. Quite a community of people living here, but she didn't feel like she was part of that community. She felt completely alone.

At the road, she turned left. Sam had turned right here before and that led to the library and a park, but today she turned left, never having gone that way before. She walked about a mile and happened upon a cemetery. It was a very well groomed cemetery, with walking paths, benches, ornate headstones. Sam wandered through it, and found a bench near a headstone for a woman named Barbara, just like her mom's name. This Barbara died in the same year that her mother had. She sat on the bench and stared at the headstone. Memories of her mom flooded over her. She remembered taking care of her mom, recalled her mom laughing and crying, and she would always remember her funeral. Sam found herself talking to this headstone... this small plot of land that now could represent her mother.

Before she knew it, the sun was going down and Sam realized that she hadn't eaten today, so she started the mile long walk back to her apartment. She took inventory of her life, as she often did, and she found a lot of emptiness. No longer married, no children, no family to speak of. Sam didn't even have a pet. She killed every house plant she's ever had, so nothing lived in her apartment except for her. And she barely lived, it seemed.

Samantha's mother passed away when she was 16. She had multiple sclerosis and had been bedridden since Sam was a young girl. Samantha grew up being the caregiver. Instead of playing dolls with her friends, she learned how to give sponge baths. Instead of playing in the neighbor's swimming pool, Sam emptied the catheter bag and tube fed her infirm mother. She escaped into books, and poured herself into school work. The year before her mother passed away, she discovered a love for poetry.

Sam's high school English teacher handed out bibles and played "Turn, Turn, Turn" by The Byrds on the record player. The class read the words along in the bible as it played, and they were taught about how inspiration for poetry can be found in many different places. Samantha went to the library after school and checked out the poetry books, what little her high school had. Sam's high school was very focused on sports, so in her mind football, basketball and track always pushed academics to the back burner.

She quickly discovered a love for Robert Frost, Anne Sexton, and Sylvia Plath. Sam yearned to live her life by taking the road less traveled as Frost instructed. In poetry, she could avoid the reality of her home life. While reading Sexton and Plath, she knew that other women had suffered. And she knew that she wasn't alone.

A few months after she turned 16, Samantha went to a school dance with her best friend, Brandy. Sam had no interest in attending a school social event, but she wanted to go to get out of the house and Brandy had wanted to go. So off to the dance they went. Sam and Brandy were each dancing in that awkward teenage way, with boys they were somewhat interested in. They made sure to stay close to one another even when dancing because it felt safe. They were interrupted and quickly dropped their hands from their partner's hips and shoulders when the principal of the school waded through the gym and swaying couples right up to Sam.

"I need you to come with me," he said. Sam looked over at Brandy, her eyes pleading for help, but Brandy wanted no part of any trouble. Samantha never questioned Brandy on that. She would have stayed back if she were in Brandy's shoes too. Sam walked into the hallway with the principal, where her cousin, Joe was standing.

"It's your mom," he said, and she followed him silently to his car. It felt like he was driving 90 miles an hour on the short drive to her house. There was an ambulance parked in the front yard, and no-one was moving. Samantha walked into the house alone. Her family members were sitting, standing.

They were silent, still, and had somehow pained and vigilant expressions like saint statues. Her mom was lying in the bed and if you couldn't feel the energy in the air, you would have assumed she was sleeping. She found out later that the ambulance workers had covered her head, but Sam's uncle had uncovered it. She looked so peaceful. Sam wandered into her grandparent's bedroom, where her aunt was on the phone, "I think she just got tired," she said.

The next week was a blur for Samantha. She picked the casket, she chose the outfit for her mom, and she asked people to sing, and to preach. Flowers had to be chosen and other preparations kept her busy. It was a matter of putting one foot in front of the other and life went on.

Sam knew that this made her different at school, she now stood out in a way that she had not asked for. She was now the girl without a mother. She had never been the popular girl at school, but this created a chasm that was absolutely uncrossable. Pity was something that Samantha had never been able to stomach, she was suspicious of anyone who tried to befriend her from that point on.

She didn't want their sympathy, she put up her walls. She built defenses that kept everyone out, and that is how she finished her high school years. She protected herself from their pity, but mostly Sam protected herself from letting people in who would only end up leaving her and breaking her heart.

Sam went to community college after high school. She floated through, not trying very hard. To any outsider, it would seem that Sam's major was in holding other's at arm's length. Samantha went through her serial-dating phase where she dated every artistic guy she could find at the community college.

Her favorite hangout became the art/music building. She dated a saxophone player named Simon, a painter named Nigel, a poet named Dave. She felt more alive around their creativity. By the end of the first year, Samantha was cutting way more classes than she was attending.

Sam dated, but she would not let anyone in. She was attracted to artists because they seemed so alive. They seemed vibrant and larger than life. She thought that their energy may rub off on her, that someday maybe she would feel something, though it never seemed to work. She would lay next to them after sex and feel more empty than ever. Samantha tried to feel what they felt. She wanted to need them, yet Sam always seemed to be withdrawing and retreating.

After her year at the community college, Sam decided to move to the big city. She got a job working as a secretary for an architect and buried herself in her work. She performed each task that was required of her, not allowing herself to think about what else was out there for her. She worked for years for the same architect and never hoped for more. Sam's existence could easily be described as grey, or two-dimensional, she did tasks assigned to her by her boss, and never questioned him. She never needed time off for any sort of social life, and Samantha never got personal calls.

Chapter 3

One day, on her break, Samantha went down to the corner coffee shop and ordered an iced mocha. She saw a familiar face, but couldn't quite place him. He was handsome, with a chiseled jaw. Sam noticed him glancing her way as well. She tried to remember where she had seen him. Perhaps he was an architect and she had seen him at meetings.

"Excuse me, do I know you?" the gentleman asked her.

"Well, you do look familiar, are you an architect?" Sam responded.

"Wait, did you go to Springfield High?" he asked.

"Oh, yes, I did. You played football, right?" Samantha replied

Sam remembered him, and she was quite shocked that he remembered her. He was Mr. Popular in high school. Sam was on the newspaper staff, a geeky young girl who was very happy to stay behind the scenes. She was the features editor, so she didn't even make football a focus of any of her writing, nor did she usually go to the games, and she had always tried to avoid the pep rallies. Sam struggled to remember his name.

"I'm John Mathews," he said.

"That's right... I'm Samantha Green," she replied

She and John visited for a few minutes when she remembered a meeting she needed to take notes for. She quickly excused herself, but before they parted, John said "would you like to go out sometime?"

"Um, sure," Sam stammered. They agreed to meet that Friday night at a Greek restaurant down the road from the coffee shop.

As she got ready for their date, Sam remembered Springfield High John. He was captain of the football team, always seemed to have a cheerleader or the prom queen on his arm. She'd pass him and his girl-du-jour in the hallways and they always seemed to be talking about either the party they were at over the weekend or the party they were going to the next weekend. They were worlds apart from Samantha and she could not imagine having anything in common with him.

Sam tried on three different outfits before deciding on one. Finally, due more to time than deciding that it was the best choice, she decided on a pair of tan slacks and a light green silk tank top. Sam brushed out her long light brown hair, applied a small amount of mascara and some lip gloss. The color of her top brought out the deep brown of her eyes. One quick last look at her reflection told her that she was as ready as she was ever going to be.

John was dressed in black slacks and a white button up shirt. He looked absolutely perfect, Sam thought. He greeted her with an awkward hug and led her into the restaurant, they were seated in a cozy candle-lit booth. They had no old times to reminisce about, so they began talking about their old town. When Samantha had left, she never looked back. John, however, had stayed for several years. Sam learned that Mr. Howell (who had owned the local hardware store) had been shot one night as he was closing his store, in an apparent robbery. She also learned that her old English teacher had been diagnosed with breast cancer and was currently fighting for her life.

It touched her, how John spoke of these tragedies, he seemed to feel them quite deeply. Sam wondered how that felt, how it would be to feel another's pain so completely. John began telling her about his family. His parents, little brother, their family electrical supply business. After telling her all about his family, he went pale and grew silent.

14

"What's wrong?" Samantha asked him.

"Here I am going on about my life and I had forgotten that you lost your mother our sophomore year. I remember hearing that news like it was yesterday, and I wanted so badly to reach out to you. I don't think you were even aware, but a group of us from school went to her funeral. We wanted to somehow be there to support you. But you were surrounded by family, and we never approached you. It was a beautiful service, and I apologize that I never took the time to tell you how sorry I was," John said.

That shook Samantha to her core. A group of people from school, people that she didn't even know had come to her mom's funeral to pay their respects to her? She couldn't even fathom that such a thing had happened.

"Thank you," she whispered.

"How did you make it through that?" John asked.

"Well, I just became preoccupied with the business of death. There is so much to be done at that time, all the arrangements, the songs, the clothes, the people. You just put one foot in front of the other, I guess," she replied.

"I watched you after that, until you left town. You were the bravest girl that I had ever seen. Such a tragedy, and you seemed to stay afloat through it all, after it all," John said.

"I didn't even have a clue that you knew who I was in high school, John. Our paths never crossed. I knew who you were, because everyone knew who you were, but how did you know me?" Sam inquired.

"I knew who you were, Sam. We met in second grade, where you would ask to go home at least three times a week and throw the biggest fits because the teacher wouldn't let you," John chuckled at the memory.

"I can't believe you remember that!" Sam said, blushing.

"I remember you all through the years. You were always quiet, always a good student, and stayed off to yourself. I always felt like you were too good for me," John admitted.

Sam pondered everything he had said. How in the world did Mr. Popular think that she was too good for him? She had always felt inadequate. She always felt like she would fall short in social situations, so she steered clear of them. Sam was from a poor family and didn't dress like the rich kids in school. She didn't socialize because she was busy taking care of her mother. Sam had always assumed the popular kids were looking down at her, so she snubbed them. She had no idea that John was admiring her from afar all those years. They each seemed lost in their own thoughts when the food arrived and they began to eat.

They enjoyed hummus with pita chips, Greek salad, and iced tea. Their conversation quickly resumed and Sam found out that John was currently a journeyman electrician, making his parents proud. She told him about her job as the architect's secretary. She told him about her boss, about the amazing buildings that he had designed. John had wired some of her bosses buildings. They both were surprised that they had never crossed paths before.

Their date was very pleasant and felt so natural, but Sam was not ready to let down any walls. She gave her number to John, but was sure that she would not hear from him again. It was alright, Sam told herself. John walked her home, and Sam was afraid that he was going to try to kiss her, afraid because then he would finally know how awkward she really was. He said good night on the sidewalk and she went back to her empty apartment.

The next morning, she slept in and made herself a bowl of oatmeal, looking over the newspaper. The sound of her phone ringing startled her.

"Hello?" Sam said into the receiver.

"Hi there! It's John. I know it may be too soon to call without seeming desperate, but I was just thinking about you, and wondered if you might want to go for a hike today," he said.

"Oh, sure, I love to hike," Sam said, stunned that he was calling her and wanted to spend time with her.

He picked her up an hour later, and they went to Silver Falls State Park to hike. John had packed a backpack lunch and knew the trails very well. They ate their lunch on a grassy hill near a waterfall while they caught their breath from the hike. Sam noticed how easy it was to be around him. Even the silence was comfortable. When John leaned in to kiss her, Sam let him. The walls that Sam had built up her whole life had started crumbling a bit for John. Samantha was not used to this feeling, she felt a connection, which was unlike anything she had ever recalled feeling before in her life.

John was gentle, caring, and extremely passionate. He was all that she had ever let herself dream of, in fact he was much more of all those things than she ever thought she deserved. Samantha and John were soon inseparable, each going out of their way to meet the other's needs, each one trying to make the other one happy. They were married six months later by a justice of the peace in a small ceremony. Sam didn't want a larger wedding, since she had no-one really to invite. She did, however, consent to a reception in their hometown, given by John's family.

Even though Sam grew up in the same town as John did, she only had a handful of people to invite to the reception.

Brandy had moved away long ago, her family: the cousins, aunts, uncles, had all lost touch. She invited her high school boss, and a couple friends. Everyone else was invited by John. Despite having only a few friends there -or perhaps because of that- Samantha had a lovely time. She didn't feel like she had gained a family, but as she made eye contact with John across the room, she knew that her husband was amazing. She felt happy through and through.

Chapter 4

During their third year of marriage, Samantha became pregnant. When she was first late for her period, John drove to the local pharmacy for an at home pregnancy test. They waited together for the results, waiting for the timer to go off. She and John were overjoyed. John told Sam how pregnancy made her glow. She was the happiest she had ever been, but many days he would catch her looking off into the distance while she washed dishes.

"Hey, Sammi, where are ya?" he would ask.

"What, hon?" Sam would reply.

"Just wondered where you are… you seem so far away," John said.

"Oh, I was just thinking. You know… just thinking," she would always answer.

What went unsaid was that she was sad every day. Sam was sad that her mom would never meet this baby. She would never get to call and ask her mom if each step of the pregnancy was normal. Her mom would never hold this child and Sam felt more alone than ever.

At the same time, Samantha bonded with this baby in ways that she never imagined possible. She would talk to the baby, and she felt more love for this one life than she had felt ever before.

When Sam first felt their child kick, she wept. She would lie in bed all day and cry. John would often come home and find her in bed, in the middle of the afternoon. John didn't know what to do. She quit her job, and John initially felt that was normal, as she was pregnant and needed time to rest. John never knew how to help Sam. He would make sure to include her in everything he planned, would plan special days, with just the two of them. Sam would put on a happy face when around other people. Sometimes, for that reason alone, John would plan activities with others, just so he could see a smile on her face.

Towards the end of her seventh month, Samantha started cramping. It was shortly after John left for work, and Sam wondered if maybe it was something she ate. By noon, though, the pain was so great that Samantha could barely stand. She sat at the table and phoned John.

"Honey, I need you," she breathed into the phone.

"What's wrong, Sam," John asked. He did not like the tone in her voice. His heart started beating faster.

"I don't know! Something's wrong," Sam cried.

John rushed home to find Sam laying in the hallway moaning. He rushed to her side, Samantha was clutching her abdomen, writhing. He immediately dialed 911, and sat on the floor with her head on his lap.

"Everything will be ok, sweetheart," John mumbled as he stroked her hair. He wasn't totally convinced, but the words still came. It seemed to take forever for the paramedics to arrive.

When they did arrive, they rushed around, setting up an IV, and for the first time, John noticed the pool of blood under Samantha. He must have gone pale, because Samantha started asking him what was wrong.

Sam was moaning and screaming "What is wrong, John? What is wrong?"

"I'm not sure honey, these men are here to help you though. You are in good hands," John said as he looked at the paramedics pleadingly.

"Ma'am, we're going to get you to the hospital. You will be well taken care of," the closest paramedic said calmly.

20

John held Sam's hand the entire ambulance ride. She sobbed uncontrollably and he wished there was something that he could do. He prayed that she would be ok, that their child would be alright. He knew how panicked she was and tried everything in his power to reassure her. He was scared though, and he felt like he had to show a brave front to her.

When they got to the hospital, they were rushed to the maternity ward, and directly into a room. The cramping had eased a bit, and Sam sobbed between the pain. The doctor came in, looking grim.

"Good afternoon, I am Dr. Hanson. I have looked at your chart, and I'd like to check you out," he said to them.

The nurses had attached a fetal heart rate monitor to her, but it didn't seem to be working right. Sam and John didn't hear the whooshing sound of their baby's heartbeat. The doctor pulled the ultrasound machine over to the bed and looked at the screen. There was no movement, no sound. They could see the baby, and it was completely still. He shook his head slightly, and looked at them with sadness in his eyes.

"I'm afraid your baby did not make it," Dr. Hanson said to them, quietly.

"There must be a mistake," John said.

Samantha wept. She had felt the absence of life. It was her worst nightmare, coming true, Sam sobbed, and she held her pregnant belly.

"Unfortunately, at this point, Samantha, you will have to expel the fetus, there is no other way," the doctor said.

John looked mortified, just as Samantha screamed from a contraction.

"The body is trying to discharge it. It will proceed just as labor does," he explained as he got his surgical gown on, "your contractions will get stronger, and I will be right here with you. When you feel like it's time to push, just push."

The urge to push came quickly, and seemed to last forever. John was aware of time much more than Samantha was, and he knew that 52 minutes had passed since they learned that the baby had died. And then he was born, if born is even the right term. John didn't know what the right term was, he just saw the still baby. The baby that he had felt kick, the baby that Samantha said ran his fist along her ribcage. A beautiful baby boy.

The doctor handed the baby to the nurses, the nurses wrapped the baby in a blue blanket and asked them if they would like to hold him. Neither of them had anticipated that. John looked at Samantha, as tears poured down her face, she nodded at him, and he held out his arms for his son.

Once the nurse placed the baby in John's arms, she quietly left the room, reminding them of the call button if they needed anything.

John held the tiny baby and rocked back and forth, sobs coming out of him. He moved to sit next to Samantha on the bed, and they both held their son, a moaning filling the room. Here was their little boy, so seemingly perfect. They were helpless, he did not make it, and neither of them understood why. They each blamed themselves.

Samantha thought about when the first cramp came, and wondered why she hadn't immediately gone to the doctor. John blamed himself for not calling the ambulance as soon as she phoned him. They were, separately, in their own personal hell. They were, together, in their collective hell.

Months later, Samantha would write the following poem, in honor of Jacob, their son.

22

For Jacob, Nevermore

I weep for you my son
I felt you growing,
moving within me,
stirring within my soul
for centuries before
you stirred in my womb.
I made you, yet….
somehow it is you that
have created us.
You shaped and formed
us into parents
then you flitted away.
Did you know we would fail?
Was your job here done?
Any possible reason
escapes through the hole left
in my heart.

      Samantha often visited Jacob's grave. Sam would go there several times a week, and sometimes stay during the entire time that John was at work. She didn't think John was even aware how often she would go there. But sometime, John would head there and see Samantha sitting there, running her fingers along the letters of his name on his headstone. He signed them both up for grief counseling, but after the third visit, Samantha said she would not go any more.

      "But why, Sammi? We need this," John asked.

      "I don't feel right going there. She doesn't know me. She just seems… well, nosey," Sam responded.

      "She can't help us if she doesn't find out who we are and what we are feeling, Sam. That's why she asks so many questions. She is trying to help us. But we have to open up in order for her to help us," John said.

It didn't seem to matter what he said, Sam just seemed to fade away more every day. He made plans at least twice a week that would involve going out with friends, as a couple. Sometimes, he would even be able to get Samantha to go. When she did, he would see small glimpses of the Sammi he knew and loved.

Chapter 6

One evening after dinner, dancing, and drinks, Sam seemed unusually happy. John fell more deeply in love with her. When they got home, John put on some soft music and held her close in a slow dance in their living room. He whispered his love to her in her ear. She looked into his eyes and began kissing him.

For the first time since Jacob, Samantha responded to his touch. Her body seemed to melt into his. John felt like he was actually connecting with her, and he never wanted this moment to end, she held his head and pulled him into her. Then she moved her hands down and started unbuttoning his shirt. John moved his hand down her back and cupped her ass, pulling her closer so she could feel his excitement.

Sam's breathing shallowed as she pulled back slightly. John pulled her blouse over her head and unfastened her bra, Sam moaned as his lips found her erect nipple. She began unbuttoning his pants and tugged them down. She squeezed him through his boxers, excited about what was to come.

John moaned. He could not believe how she was responding to him. It had been so long. He pulled her skirt down, leaving her in only her black panties.

She pulled John's boxers off, freeing his engorged member. He kissed her hungrily as she began stroking him. His right hand was squeezing her ass and his left hand was kneading her nipple. Sam whispered into John's ear, "I want you." Hearing that, he could wait no longer. He laid her on the rug and entered her. He kissed her deeply as he thrust. She grabbed onto his ass, pulling him in closer.

Sam's body seemed to have a life of it's own, gone was all the sadness she had been carrying around for months, years even. Now she couldn't get enough of John. She wanted to pull him inside her more. If she could have devoured him, she would have. Sam needed John to feel her, to be inside her. She raised her legs and put them on his shoulders as he pushed further and further inside her. She moaned with orgasm after orgasm.

He moved inside her slowly, enjoying the feeling of that slow, controlled movement. Sam came to, grabbing his hips and pulling him in hard. She arched her back and moaned, feeling another orgasm coming. She grunted with her orgasm, and she could feel a wet spot below her on the rug. She yelled out "I love you, John" as she came again. She could feel him swell as he grunted, and she knew that he was right there with her, at the same time.

John lowered himself on top of her, kissing her. She held him close. He rolled onto his back, pulling her on top of him and he felt the tears roll off of her face onto his chest. He held her tight until she seemed to fall asleep. He didn't want the moment to end, John wanted his wife back. He wanted her to feel, to be able to love, to make love, and be passionate. The tears told him that she was fading away again. He led her into the bedroom and kissed her good night as he held her. John prayed that tomorrow the happy Samantha would still be there with him.

When he woke, Samantha was gone. He knew, without a doubt, that she had gone to the cemetery. John decided to join her, he wanted to grieve with her, to let her know that he was in this too. He had lost not only a son, but a wife. When he got there, she was tracing Jacob's name with her finger, tears streaming down her face. John walked up behind Samantha and held her tight.

"I miss him too, Sam," John said.

"I just don't know what to do," Sam replied.

"Neither do I sweetheart, but I do know that we can't make it without each other," he said.

Sam turned to him, looked deep into his eyes, wiped his tears, and hugged him. "John, I think I need to get a job. I need to do something to get out of the house. I need something to help give me purpose," she said. He simply nodded.

Chapter 7

Two weeks later, Sam started her new job at the assisted living facility. She had no prior work experience in this field. However, when she talked about her childhood in which she was a main caregiver for her mother, Jack, the administrator, could tell that she would be a good fit.

Samantha's first month at the assisted living was very rocky, she was very soft-spoken and the residents had a hard time hearing her. Sam seemed so unsure of herself and didn't assert herself well. Jack had received many complaints about her, but he had a feeling that she would thrive in this job. He had a feeling that both Sam and the residents would benefit from her being here. Jack assigned Sam to shower duty. He had put together a schedule for all of the residents who needed help, and told Sam that it was her job to get the showers done that were assigned to her shift.

The first day as shower aide, Samantha had to log several refusals into the residents' books. The two that she had successfully assisted with were difficult for her. She ended up every bit as wet as the residents who were showering. On her third shower aide shift, Jack called her into his office.

"I've noticed a lot of refusals this week," he said to her.

"They don't want to shower, Jack, I don't know what to do," Samantha replied.

"Ok, so we need to talk about a few things. First of all, the residents must bathe regularly. If they aren't clean, we're opening them up to skin breakdown, infections, they will smell bad, and their families will think we are not taking good care of them," Jack said.

"I know all of that, Jack. But I go in, tell them I'm there to assist them, and they just say no," Sam said.

"Well, we need to consider why it is they say no. Showers may take a lot of their energy, and be an exhausting experience for them. They may feel unstable on their feet, and be afraid of getting hurt. They may be modest and not like to undress in front of someone. They may have scars, saggy skin, mastectomies, so many qualities that they perceive unattractive. I'd like you to find out how to overcome all of these things. If you think they are modest, find a way to reassure them, and be as respectful as possible while getting your job done. If you think it's exhausting, schedule their shower right before bed, or before a nap. If they are unstable, find ways to make it safe for them, and let them know you are doing so" Jack said.

"By this time next week, I want to see minimal refusals. I'm assigning this job to you, Sam, because I know that you are capable," he said

"Thank you, Jack, I will do my best," She said.

That night, after dinner, Sam sat on the couch with John and told him about the tasks Jack had assigned her. She told him about the challenges before her, about some of the ways that she would solve some of the problems. John watched her with such astonishment, he saw that some sadness was still there. Sam had developed some frown lines, a few wrinkles, but she seemed to be alive again. He watched as she wrote list after list of each resident and their issues. She noted who would need a nap or bedtime after a shower, who would be uneasy on their feet. She used a coded worksheet to protect their identity, Sam was so conscious of their rights and not getting information out.

Sam went online and searched for photos. She looked at mastectomy scars, scars on elderly bodies who had abdominal surgery, photos of amputations and every sort of disfigurement she could think of that may apply to her residents. She prepared herself so that there would be no surprise in her eyes, only complete acceptance. She had listed some illnesses so that she could become more familiar. She learned about COPD, and the need for a shower chair so that rest could be had in the middle of a shower. She even read about the challenges of obesity, and the areas that could not be reached easily and made notes about tools that could be made to help them to wash themselves. She read about skin folds, and bacteria that get caught, yeast infections, all the problems related. She went from website to website to look at tools available for the elderly population. She printed out lists, and made notes.

When Sam went to work the next day, she spent her break time in Jack's office, showing him what she had learned. She told him that her next step was to go from resident to resident and ask them when it is they want their shower, what their concerns are. It was important to her that the residents would be heard, Sam wanted the residents to be part of the decision making.

"I am so impressed with all that you have done, Sam. I will clear your schedule to ensure that you are free to get this straightened out. Thank you so much," Jack said.

Samantha left Jack's office feeling accomplished, but knew there was so much work to be done. She went to the break room to compile a list of residents to interview. Some, with dementia, she would have to interview with families present in order to get complete information. She made a list of questions, had Jack approve them, and made copies. Then she began. She perused their charts to fill out the questions she could answer regarding their diagnosis. She answered questions about when their current shower is scheduled, what staff they refused, and what staff they had allowed to shower them. Then she interviewed staff members to see what worked for them in the past. She wanted the most comprehensive information that she could have.

The next day, Sam began interviewing the residents. She talked with them alone, in their rooms, and it was a slow process. She had to make sure they were completely comfortable with her. Once she had their trust, she believed she could make the shower schedule work for them. Sam learned that even the most quiet residents had something to say. They knew who they liked and who they trusted. They were very particular about the time of day, the temperature of the water, which towels were used. There was very little that they didn't have an opinion about, she learned. Before now, nobody had asked what it was that they preferred. They just slapped their names on the shower schedule and barged in to get the job done.

The act of listening was probably Sam's best ally. The residents felt like no-one cared. They were gathered up and fed as a group, they were marched around, even gotten up on someone else's schedule. By the week's end, Samantha had a shower schedule in place, and there were minimal refusals. Jack noticed the changes in the residents and asked Sam to train the staff in their monthly staff meetings. Sam's efforts were also noticed by their facility RN, Sandra. Sandra cornered Samantha one day at lunch time.

"Why have you never pursued nursing?" Sandra asked her.

"Well, I have thought about it, but I didn't really think that it was a good fit for me," Sam replied.

"When you are ready, Sam, I will help you in any way that I can. You would make an excellent nurse," Sandra told her.

That night, over dinner, Samantha told John what Sandra had said to her.

"You know, Sam, if that's what you want, I'll support you," John said.

"I'm not sure what I want, to tell you the truth," she replied.

"You will. There's no rush, sweetheart," John said.

The longer Samantha worked at the assisted living facility, the more sure she was that this was the right path for her. She was meant to be a caregiver. She had never told anyone, but she felt that it was her calling in life to be a healer of some sort. Right now, giving the residents a place to be heard, this was where she was supposed to be.

In a way, doing this job, and doing it well, helped Samantha to feel like her childhood all happened for a reason. Perhaps the reason was to help her to be a good caregiver, to have empathy and understanding with people who usually are not afforded such things.

Chapter 8

One day, towards the end of her shift, a co-worker, Katie, asked Sam if she'd like to go to a painting class with her. It was the next weekend, and they both happened to have the day off.

"I've never painted in my life," Sam told her.

"That doesn't matter! Come and try it out, see what you think. I discovered painting a few years ago and it has really helped me. It gave me something to pour myself into and made me feel worthy, if that makes any sense," Katie replied.

Sam agreed to go with her, but it made her very nervous. She had never considered herself artistic, and felt like she would surely fail in this group of people. No doubt they all had artistic abilities oozing out of their pores!

Saturday mornings were lazy mornings for Sam and John. They slept in, drank their coffee on the deck, and usually just lounged for much of the day. Sometimes they would cuddle up and watch movies, or they would clean the house and catch up on chores. John used to go golfing on the weekends, but since Jacob he has given it all up to stick closer to home, to keep an eye on Samantha.

When Sam came home and told John about the painting class, he was surprised. He never knew that she wanted to paint. He had never really known her to have girlfriends, nor had he known her to break routine. John, however, was also thrilled. He was excited that Sam was branching out, and secretly he was relieved and made plans to go golfing with some coworkers.

After their leisurely coffee on the deck, they showered together and each got ready for their day. John chuckled as Sam went through several outfits. She finally decided on old, broken in jeans and a sweater, with a scarf. She felt it was artsy, but not so nice that she'd worry about ruining it. John kissed her goodbye when Katie came to pick her up. He could tell that she was nervous, but he also noticed a gleam in her eye that he had not seen for a very long time.

The painting class was offered by the community college, and it was being held at an elementary school. Sam was auditing this class as a guest, but she knew the door was wide open if she liked it, and she could continue. It was an Oil Painting Basics class. Sam and Katie walked in, a bit early, and there were 20 or so easels set up all over the room. Each one had a canvas on it and a smock laying across the canvas. Katie led her to the right spot and they each put a smock on.

The teacher, Glenda, came over to speak to the ladies.

"Hi there Katie! So nice to see you! And thank you for bringing a friend! Hi there, I'm Glenda, and I'll be your instructor," she said.

"Pleased to meet you, I'm Samantha. Please call me Sam," she responded.

"Have you ever painted before, Sam?" Glenda asked.

"No, I never have," Sam admitted.

"Good! I'm glad to hear that! No bad habits to unteach!" Glenda laughed. "You'll do just fine! The best thing about painting is that as you learn new techniques, you can paint right over your previous work if you'd like," Glenda replied.

During the class, they covered their canvases with gesso and talked a bit about what they'd like to paint. Glenda wanted them to pick their subject and she would teach techniques accordingly. One of the ladies had brought a bouquet of flowers and Samantha chose to paint a group of daisies, her favorite flower.

Sam learned how to mix her oil paints with gel medium, how to mix colors, how to layer colors on the canvas. She felt transported to a whole new world. Pretty soon, she was painting petals. She painted white petals, with a bright yellow center. Having never used oil paints before, she had not realized that the paints would blend for days, and she had not painted a background. Samantha wanted a dark blue background. After she talked to Glenda, she got a fresh canvas and applied gesso to it. She painted the background a deep blue, mixing in some light blue and some purple, brushing it in, creating depth.

Sam looked at her canvas, and she was in love. The beauty and the depth of the background alone made her want to weep. Samantha was hooked. She would have to wait until next week for it to be dry enough to paint her daisies. She assured Katie and Glenda that she would be back!

That evening, after dinner, Samantha told John that she'd like to buy some supplies. She wanted to set up her own painting area at home, so that she didn't have to wait a whole week to try some new ideas she had. Several hours later, they were leaving the craft store with a large amount of supplies. Sam had her own easel, several blank canvases, brushes, oil paints, turpentine, a brush basin, a palette, and lots of gel medium. Oh, and gesso, of course!

John was amazed at the changes he saw in Samantha. She was glowing, and bubbling over with excitement. Samantha got up early Sunday morning and set up her easel on the deck. She had applied gesso to a couple canvases the night before. She and John still had coffee on the deck, but it was as she was painting. John fell in love with her all over again as he watched her put yellows and reds across the canvas. He could tell that it was a sunset. John was amazed that Samantha already had the ability to create such beauty, after just one class.

Lunch time rolled around and John went to see what Sam was doing. He was delighted to see that she was still painting. Samantha had four canvases in process at this point, each one vastly different from the others. Each one was amazingly beautiful. John prepared a couple of salads and some iced tea, and took lunch out to the deck.

Samantha looked up at John with the plates in his hands. She looked shocked.

"Oh, I'm so sorry, John. I didn't realize it was already lunch time!" Samantha said.

"It's perfectly alright, babe," John said, "you were obviously busy! Tell me about your paintings while we eat, will you?"

"Ok, thank you. Lunch looks wonderful! The one with the gold and red is a sunset," Samantha explained, "I'll have to layer the colors, so none are complete yet. The dark blue background will be a cityscape, with skyscrapers and the glow of the city night. The one with pale pinks and blues will be a sunrise. And I think the green one will just be an abstract, but I can't really know for sure yet," Samantha laughed.

"They are already so beautiful, Sam," John said, and Samantha could tell that he really meant it. She glowed with accomplishment and pride.

Chapter 9

"Let's go out tonight, John," Sam said, surprising him.

"Absolutely, hon! Let's make a night of it, shall we?" he responded.

Sam took an unusually long time getting ready and John began to fear that she had changed her mind. She had not instigated a date since before Jacob's birth. He had been holding back, allowing her to set the pace. How does one heal after losing part of their soul? Each time he tried to control the situation, by forcing grief counseling for instance, she withdrew. However, when he stepped back, she made choices: went back to work, started painting, and healing began. He was in awe of this woman, and fell more in love with her every day.

John could feel his jaw drop as Sam walked into the room. She was wearing a beige sundress that hugged her every curve. She seemed to glow, was so full of life. He knew that with each step she chose, she was healing. John wanted nothing more than his vibrant, loving wife back.

"You look amazing, hon," John said.

Samantha blushed and spun in a circle in front of him.

They went to happy hour at their neighborhood bar. Samantha ordered a lemon drop and John a rum and coke. They were lucky enough to live within walking distance from their favorite bar, restaurant, and nightclub. After one drink, Sam began flirting with John, running her toes along his leg under the table as she talked to him.

Dinner went by quickly, with each of them eating salad and a bacon wrapped filet. John noticed that Sam had a voracious appetite, which made him happy. She had been losing weight since Jacob's birth... since his death. The memories flooded back to him. Holding his son, his son who never took a breath. He didn't even realize that there was a tear running down his cheek until Sam rushed over to him.

"Oh sweetheart," she said as she pulled his head into her chest.

"I'm ok, Sammi, was just remembering," John said.

"Do you want to go home, love?" she asked, looking into his eyes.

"We've been having such an amazing night, I don't want to ruin it," John responded.

"Shhh... let's get out of here, we've had a wonderful night, we are just choosing to continue it at home, alright?" Sam said as she signaled to the waiter to bring their check.

They walked home, hand in hand, clutching onto one another, as if their lives depended on it. When they got into the living room, John grabbed her into a tight hug, squeezing her so hard that she felt like he was going to cut off her breathing. She felt his body start to heave, she felt the sobs bubble up from deep within him, she heard the anguish come out of his body. The sound was one that would haunt her for years, a sound that seemed otherworldly. They crumpled onto the couch, John wailing, Sam holding him tight.

John sobbed for over an hour. Then he drifted off, into a deep sleep. Sam stroked his hair as he slept. She had only seen him cry once before, and that was the day Jacob died. That day, he wailed then too, she realized. The loss was so great. Had he been holding it all in this whole time? Yes, she realized, he had. All of a sudden, he shook awake, his eyes wide.

"Oh my god, I'm so sorry. We were having an amazing night and I totally ruined it," he gasped.

"Oh stop, our night is not ruined. I was thinking of lighting some candles, putting some music on, pouring some wine... what do you think?" Sam asked.

"I do love you. You know that, right?" John asked, while looking deep into her eyes.

"Yes, of course I do," she responded as she leaned forward to kiss him.

They each seemed starved for touch, John opened his lips as hers touched his, darting his tongue towards hers. Sam tilted her head and opened her mouth wider, allowing him entrance. She became wet with longing as he put his hand on the back of her head, pulling her further into him.

"I want you, Sam," John breathed into her.

Sam reached down and caressed John's chest, then his thigh, lightly rubbing his body, knowing she was making him crazy. She could tell that he wanted nothing more than for her to pull his pants off. She knew this, and she chose to drive him mad for a while longer. He kept trying to pull her into him, she resisted, touching him lightly, kissing him slowly. Each time he tried to speed up the pace, she slowed it down. He growled as he kissed her.

"I ache for you," John said, barely above a whisper.

Sam said nothing in response, instead she simply moved her hand down his chest and slipped it into his pants. She deepened her kisses as she began stroking him. He moaned, and began kissing her more hungrily, like he wanted to devour her right there.

"I think we need to forget about the candles," John said as he stood up, "let's go to our room, shall we?"

Sam followed behind him, her hand in his back pocket. When they reached the bedroom, John turned to her and enveloped her in his arms as he began kissing her deeply. He reached down to her waist, then pulled the dress up over her head. He was pleased to see she had nothing on underneath it but his favorite red g-string. What a sly devil, he thought... she was planning a seduction.

"I am one lucky man," John said as he put his thumbs in each side of the panties and pulled them down. Samantha stepped out of the g-string as she pulled his shirt off of him. She then pulled him over to the bed and on top of her.

They moved in unison, satisfying their needs and desires until they fell into a deep sleep in one another's arms.

"Good morning, my love," John said as Sam opened her eyes while he walked into the bedroom carrying her breakfast in. Sam sat up in bed, smiling at John, who was only wearing boxers, and who had apparently made her an entire breakfast. On the plate was bacon, eggs, toast, jam, and he was carrying a large glass of orange juice.

"Wow, hon, thank you so much! Are you going to eat with me?" Sam asked.

"Sure am, just have to grab my plate!" John replied. John re-entered the room holding an identical meal to Sam's and sat next to her on the bed. "Thank you so much for last night, Sam," he said.

"You don't have to thank me, it was amazing," Sam responded.

"Well, yes, the sex was... but I meant before that. When I had my meltdown," John said, avoiding eye contact as he replied.

"Oh, sweetie, we all have meltdowns. I realized last night that you have been holding in all your emotions, always putting me and my feelings first. We both lost a son. The rug was pulled out from under both of us. We prepared for a time of joy, we were multiplying our love. His death divided us. Your 'meltdown' as you called it was a long time coming," Sam said as she looked into his eyes, "this breakfast is amazing, by the way."

"Thank you," John said, "what would you like to do today?"

Sam looked down at her plate and answered quietly, "I was hoping to paint, actually, if that is ok with you."

John finished his last bite and jumped up off of the bed. "Of course, sweetheart! I was hoping to go fishing, if you don't mind."

"I don't mind a bit, you made breakfast though, so leave the dishes for me," Sam replied.

"I wouldn't dream of depriving you of that joy!" John said with a laugh, "I will be home by dinner. Maybe we can grill some burgers?"

"Sounds perfect! Have a great time fishing!" Sam said as he walked out of the room.

Chapter 10

A day spent painting was Sam's idea of heaven. She had one canvas with a dark background all ready for it's next layer. That one, though, Sam put off, instead, she worked on one that was split in the middle. On top, she painted oranges and browns, while on bottom she put blues and greens. She pictured an ocean sunset, and really it looked amazing. It was far from done, but beautiful already. She glared at the dark canvas, "ok, now I guess I have to get to you."

Sam wiped her palette clean and looked at her color options. On the palette she put yellow paint, brown, black, a dab of white. She took a deep breath and began mixing colors. She put yellow on the edge of the brush, then brown, all mixed together, with the yellow still there. Then she put the brush on the canvas. This one wasn't like the others. This one she had not planned. She simply wanted to paint something that represented her, something that showed who she was. She began painting, and even though she had no idea what was going to happen, she painted for an hour. When she was done, she stepped back to look at it.

Sam gasped as she saw the painting. The entire thing was so dark. Is this what she had become? The background was dark, almost black, with a swirl covering the entire painting, from the outside corner, round and round and round till a dark core. The swirl was brown, yellow, tiny bit of white, but at parts of the painting was imperceptible from the background. Sam understood this painting. She had been spiraling into darkness since Jacob's death. Tears rolled down her face. Of course, at that very moment, John walked in.

"Hey hon, what's going on? Is everything alright?" John asked after he noticed her tears.

"What? Oh yeah, I'm fine. Was just finishing up this painting," Sam said, "are you hungry? I could start up the grill!"

"I'll start the grill, you finish what you were doing. Are you sure everything is ok?" John asked, suspiciously.

"Yeah, I was just thinking about some things, that's all. Mostly about how different we are now, after Jacob's...." Sam trailed off.

"We aren't the same people, I agree. If I could change things, you know I would, hon," John said.

"Let's start dinner. No sense dwelling in the past now," Sam replied.

They were both quiet all throughout dinner prep. Each lost in their own thoughts. John was wondering if Sam was going to slip away again, Sam was wondering if that darkness inside of her would ever go away, or rather, she wondered if it would take over her life. She had no idea how to convey any of this to John, nor was she sure that she wanted to.

At dinner, to lighten the mood, John started one of their favorite conversations, "Hey hon, if we won the lottery tomorrow, where would you want to go first?"

"Um... I think first I would want to travel to Egypt to see the pyramids, how about you?" Sam replied.

"I'll give my answer in a minute, but why Egypt? I didn't know that you were interested in the pyramids," John said.

"Oh, one of the residents was talking about a trip to Egypt the other day when I was helping him. He made it sound so magical. I would love to go there for the history alone, but there is also apparently is such a culture there. Wouldn't you love to go into a pyramid?" Sam answered.

"Well, you've pretty much convinced me," John said, laughing, "I was going to say Venice. I would love to take you on a gondola ride."

"Oh wow, that would be lovely! We likely wouldn't come home for a very long time, if we planned to go to all the places that we would enjoy. France, England, Germany, the Great Wall of China!" Sam said, excitedly, "where would you like to live should we win the lottery?"

"I would like to live out in the country, on some acreage, with a farmhouse, some outbuildings, a cellar, some fruit trees, and a creek running through the property. If there are salmon in that creek, then even better!" John replied, laughing.

"Wow, that does sound like a little slice of heaven! We could have a garden and a clothesline!" Sam said, laughing, "oh listen to me, I don't sound like a millionaire do I?"

"I don't think our dreams would change. We've always wanted that simple life, we would just be able to attain it sooner! And travel a lot, but maybe in the rainy, non gardening months," John replied, winking at her.

"Oh, of course! No-one wants to spend all nine rainy months of the year in the Pacific Northwest! Maybe we could have a winter home in... Paris?" Samantha said.

"Absolutely! Or we could just travel. Paris, Sidney, somewhere in Thailand, Asia, I've heard you will even be able to book trips to the moon soon!" John replied.

"Uh... if space travel is what you're after, then you'll be going alone, mister," Samantha retorted.

"Oh, alright, to the moon alone. But you'd better have your passport ready for all the other travels!" he responded, "how about we have some wine on the deck? It's such a beautiful evening."

Sam grabbed a bottle of wine and John took the glasses outside. They sat, looking up at the stars and planning their trips around the globe until the wine was long gone and they were each yawning.

"I think it's time that I took my bride to bed," John said as he stood up, extending his hand to Sam. Sam simply nodded in agreement, smiling at him. She was feeling a bit tipsy and was thankful for the support. After placing their glasses in the sink, John escorted her to the bedroom. Sam was sound asleep by the time he turned off the lights. He kissed her forehead before rolling over to sleep. His biggest hope was that she wouldn't have any nightmares tonight. Sam had been having nightmares several times a week now since Jacob died. She seemed to be doing better lately but he had caught her crying earlier. He was worried about her. He couldn't afford to have her slip away from him again.

Sam woke up screaming at 3:15am. It was always the same. She would start by thrashing around, mumbling, then she would sit up abruptly, screaming "no" over and over. John would hold her tight, waking her gently. This night was no different. Screaming, waking, then quiet for a moment, a gasp, then sobbing, every time. And each time John's heart broke a little more. She would never tell him what the dreams were about, but he knew she was reliving that day, the day she gave birth. They had talked about trying again, but Sam always simply said she wasn't ready. John felt like a healthy baby would help them so much. They each had so much love to give and they would make wonderful parents. Of course, he understood that she couldn't face the possibility of that loss again.

Sam never seemed to fully wake up after these nightmares. Each time after sobbing, she would just start this light snoring that always seemed to put John's mind at ease. He would lower her back down to her pillow and cover her before rolling on his side, trying to resume sleep. Often, he would spend hours trying to figure out how to fix everything. And more often than not, he came up empty.   If he could figure out how to fix everything, he would.

Chapter 11

"Jack, I'm in room 202, Rodney is seizing, 911 has been called," Sam said to Jack, knowing that if the paramedics showed up he would wonder. She didn't even hear him respond, she didn't have time. She had been going by his room to give Ada a shower when she heard a banging sound coming from Rodney's room. Rodney was their youngest tenant, and he was there after some extensive drug use, which left him brain damaged. Sam used her key and as soon as she opened the door, she saw him, he was on his side on the carpet and it looked like he had been seizing for a while. Rodney's ankle was rubbed raw from the movement on the carpet. She called 911, and worked to change his position a bit so that no further damage was done. Then she waited.

It seemed like forever, but she knew that only a few minutes had passed. The paramedics always put Samantha's mind at ease, each of them moving in, each knowing what role to play. Every team she saw worked like a well oiled machine. Sam loved their lack of emotion, their precision. She watched them work until they rolled the gurney into the ambulance. Then she walked down to Jack's office.

"Jack, I got ahold of Rodney's sister and she will be meeting him at the hospital. I found some empty beer bottles in his closet, so likely he was drinking again. And with his medication.... well, we had told him what would happen. Dammit, he promised not to drink," Sam said, exasperated and exhausted.

"You did great, Sam, go take a break. As long as you'd like," Jack said, "thank you for taking care of everything, you always go above and beyond," Jack responded.

Rodney didn't have many friends, so she didn't need to inform the residents of his hospital visit. However, she went and talked to Sandra, who she knew would be in the nurse's station. Sandra didn't even look up when Sam walked in.

"I knew you'd be in here to see me. You know there was nothing we could have done to prevent this, right? We are not a lockdown facility. Our residents are free to come and go as they wish. We talked to Rodney about the risks and he made his choices," Sandra said.

"My mind knows all that," Sam replied, "but I just wish..."

"It was his choice. Rodney had some brain damage, yes, but he had enough cognitive ability to make decisions. He chose to drink, and unfortunately that decisions has some possibly fatal consequences," Sandra replied.

"Do you think he will die?" Sam asked, her voice catching.

"Based on past experience, yes, I do. He could surprise me and rally but I'm not sure that he can make it back from this one. We don't know how long he had been seizing. We don't know how much he had been drinking, or for how long. I will be surprised if he pulls through. I know that's not what you want to hear, and I'm sorry. But you did an amazing job. You called 911 immediately. He could have still been up in his room had you not stopped and checked on him. Jack even tells me that you contacted his sister as well. You do good work, and these residents are lucky to have you!" Sandra said, walking over to pat Sam on the shoulder.

Sam looked at her watch. Rodney was transported an hour ago. She wondered if there was any news, but realized that it was unlikely to hear anything this soon. She probably wouldn't hear any updates until tomorrow since her shift was almost over.

Chapter 12

Sam was always glad that she got home an hour before John. That way she had a chance to unwind, shower if she needed to, and be calm and personable by the time he got home. Some days it was really easy to prepare herself, but days like today, that were emotionally draining, were harder to bounce back from. She didn't like for him to worry, so she always made sure to freshen her makeup and put a smile on her face. Sometimes though, Sam felt like she was struggling to hold it all together, and today was one of those days.

"Hon, are you home?" John yelled as he walked in the door.

"Yeah, I'm outside, painting! Dinner is in the oven," Samantha hollered back.

John joined her outside with some drinks after he hung up his jacket.

"How was your day?" he asked, noting the dark circles under her eyes.

"It was long, honestly, one of the residents is in the hospital. I found him seizing," Sam replied.

"Wow, really sorry to hear that hon. I'm sure you did all you could do, is he going to be ok?" John asked.

"Sandra doesn't think he will make it," Sam whispered.

John walked over and wrapped his arms around her. Despite all of her preparations, Sam burst into tears and sobbed into his shoulder. John held her as she cried. He worried at times that the job was too much for her but she seemed to love it. Once again, he felt helpless and unsure. John figured he couldn't go wrong if he kept holding her, so that's what he did. After a while, Sam pulled her head back to look into John's eyes.

"Thank you for always being here, no matter what," she said to him.

He simply leaned in to kiss her.

"Dinner's ready!" Samantha said, wiping her tears.

"Why don't you take the salads out to the table outside and I will bring the casserole. When we are done eating, you can continue painting and I'll bring my laptop out to get a bit of work done," John suggested.

John poured wine as Sam served up the salad. She had made Greek salad, just like they enjoyed on their first date. The casserole was chicken, rice, and broccoli with cheese. They ate mostly in silence, savoring the flavors.

"I made enough so we could take it for lunches or have leftovers sometime this week," Sam said.

"Oh, that's a great idea! I think I'll put it in individual servings when I clear the table, then we can go from there," John replied.

Sam enjoyed the fact that he helped her around the house. He started helping more after Jacob and Sam sometimes felt like he was just babying her because he thought she was going to break. Nonetheless, she enjoyed the help so she didn't often question it. If she were being honest with herself, she was feeling much less fractured these days. She had days that she missed her mom still, and days she wondered what Jacob would look like or be doing right now. More often than not, though, each day was good.

Chapter 13

Sam loved her job and felt like she was making a difference most days. However, there were days that Sam had to argue with Ethel about testing her blood sugar before meals. Those days, when Ethel crossed her arms over her ample bosom, glared at Sam and told her that she was tired of being a pincushion, those days were not Sam's favorite, but she had just the right amount of stubborn to be on the receiving end of Ethel's tantrum.

"I understand, Ethel. I really do. Every single day, at least three times a day, we stab you in the finger and squeeze a drop of blood out. I know it hurts. And you know as well as I do that it is necessary. We can't serve you until this is done and your insulin has been administered," Sam would tell her.

Some days, Ethel would march out to her table in the dining room, banging her fist on the table saying "serve me now!" The staff, however, knew to wait for the go-ahead from the med-aide on duty. Sam would simply shake her head when they turned to her. Ethel would glare. A few minutes later, Ethel would come back to the medication room. She wouldn't speak, she would just sit down and put her finger out for Sam to poke.

"I'm sorry, this is going to hurt," Sam would say and she tried to be as gentle as possible, but when you are basically stabbing someone, gentleness is not an option.

"Dammit, that hurts!" Ethel would yell.

"I know it does... I wish we didn't have to do it, but we've got to keep you healthy so you can take Boo on walks, don't we?" Sam would respond.

Ethel loved her dog Boo. Sam had thought more than once if it weren't for that dog, Ethel wouldn't have the will to live. Sam knew how to stay on Ethel's good side (if she had one). She brought treats to Boo and always asked Ethel if Boo needed anything.

"I'm not above bribery, John," Sam said that evening to John as she told him about her day.

"I guess that's good, whatever works," he said, laughing. "Hey, have you thought any more about becoming a nurse? You certainly have the skills for it, not bribery, all of the other stuff, the way that you interact with the residents."

"It's been in the back of my mind, but I haven't thought a lot about it. Can we afford for me to go to school full time? I just don't know that now is the best time," Sam said, dismissively.

"Hon, if it is something you want to do, we will figure it out. You would qualify for grants. We have some money in savings. Perhaps it would be difficult at times, considering finances and stress involved, but I think it would be doable if you decide that's what you want to do," John said.

"I know. I will think about it," Sam replied, "would you like to order in tonight or go to the cafe? We both worked late and I'm exhausted, I'm sure you are too."

"Let's order Chinese tonight. I will go pick it up. Should I get our usual?" John replied.

"Oh! That sounds great! I will get out the plates and chopsticks while you are gone. What would you like to drink tonight? I was thinking rum and cokes," Sam said.

"Sounds perfect! I will call the order in now and it will be ready by the time I get there. I will be back soon, why don't you relax for a bit. If there is anything to be done around the house, we can deal with it later," John said as he grabbed his keys and cell phone.

Sam decided to take a quick shower and freshen up. She hadn't been home very long and always liked to wash any work smells off of her and get her clothes in the laundry. After the shower, she gathered up all the laundry from the upstairs. As she was walking down the stairs, she got extremely dizzy and lost her footing. She tumbled down the stairs, with nothing but the laundry breaking her fall. She was stunned, and it took her a moment to catch her breath, but she did an assessment and nothing was broken. She felt her face, and didn't feel any bruising. She looked behind her at the stairs and felt the bottom one. Sam had never realized before how padded they were. Her heart was beating at a rapid pace and she wondered what caused that. John would be home shortly though, and she felt the strong desire to not be on the floor when he came home. He worried so much already.

Sam gathered the laundry and started the washing machine. Her mind was reeling, but she assumed this was an isolated incident. Perhaps her toe had caught on the stair, no, she had felt dizzy first. She busied herself with making the drinks as John returned.

"Hey hon, I think you dropped a sock by the stairs," he said as he walked by.

"Oh, shoot, I guess I did. You know how hard it is to hold on to all the laundry when you bring it down!" Sam said as she picked it up and carried it to the washer. "Have a seat, John, everything should be on the table!"

"I love Pagoda, they always have such good food," John gushed as they ate.

"Mmmmhmmm," was all Sam said, her mouth full.

They ate mostly in silence, each devouring the food on their plate.

"Wow, we were hungry... guess we shouldn't eat so late!" Sam said, "what does your fortune say?"

John smiled broadly and read "'money will come to you when you are doing the right thing'... in bed. What does yours say?"

"Mine says 'be assertive when decisive action is needed'...in bed," Sam said, giggling.

"You get to be assertive in bed... but what I do in bed will make me rich," John said.

"Only if you do the right thing!" Sam belted out, laughing so hard she was gasping for breath.

"Hey, what do you think about getting in the hot tub? May be a nice way to finish the night," John suggested.

"That sounds heavenly. I'll get the towels, will you refill our drinks?" Sam said as she headed to the linen closet. On her way there, she heard a distinct sound, like someone had a thin piece of metal and pinged it, then the room spun. She grabbed onto the wall to brace herself. She was so dizzy, she had no idea where the wall was and banged her hand into it as she tried to steady herself. John heard the noise and came running.

"Are you alright, hon? What happened?" he asked breathlessly as he reached out to hold her.

"Oh, I just got a little dizzy, I'm alright," Sam answered, trying to act nonchalant.

"Well, your hand doesn't look alright, it is probably going to bruise and you have a bit of a scrape," John said, "are you sure you are up to sitting in the hot tub?"

Samantha took a deep breath, "Yeah, I'm sure that it was just a fluke, all is well, and the hot tub will be so relaxing."

That night, as John lay in bed next to her, Samantha was wide awake, wondering what was going on. She had thought that falling down the stairs was an act of clumsiness, however, she remembered feeling dizzy just prior. Then it happened again within a couple hours. Perhaps she had an ear infection. Dizziness is often a symptom of that. She decided she would have Sandra look in her ears tomorrow at work.

Even though she had a possible explanation for her dizzy spells, Sam tossed and turned until morning. What if it wasn't an ear infection? She thought about getting out of bed and taking her temperature but didn't want to disturb John by getting up. She remembered that her leg was tingling when she got up from her fall earlier.

"Oh, Sam, stop it!" she thought to herself, "you are just imagining things now. It was simple vertigo."

Chapter 14

The next day at work, Sam spent her break talking to Sandra. She told her about the two bouts of dizziness, about hearing a metallic twang just prior to the room spinning.

"So you fell down the stairs?" Sandra asked as she looked at Sam's elbows and knees.

"Yes, but I was holding an armful of laundry plus our stairs are really padded. Nothing is broken." Sam responded.

"Have you been doing anything differently? Has your diet changed? Your sleep patterns? Your stress levels?" Sandra asked, removing the thermometer from Sam's mouth.

"No, nothing is different. Life is always stressful, isn't it? But I've been painting, and John is so attentive. There aren't any stressors recently, no," Sam replied.

"Your ears look clear, no sign at all of an ear infection. If this happens again, you will need to do two things. First of all, write down what happened immediately prior. Everything. Feelings, sounds, smells, stressors, food you ate, any tingling in your limbs. Second, take all the information to your doctor. This could be nothing, but if it continues it could be extremely serious," Sandra told her.

"Sandra, my mom had MS... " Sam said, trailing off.

"I know, Sam, given your family history, that's more of a reason to be concerned. Like I said, it could be nothing, though, so don't dwell on this. This could be the very last time," Sandra reassured her.

"Thank you Sandra. I really appreciate your time. Have you heard anything about Rodney?" Sam asked her.

"Last I heard, he still hadn't woken up. I'm sorry, but it's not looking good," Sandra said.

"Oh dear, maybe I will go visit again, I bet his sister could use a break," Sam replied.

Work was uneventful and afterwards she went straight to the hospital to see Rodney. Sam wasn't prepared for how Rodney looked today. He seemed so swollen, and he had started turning a shade of green.

"Thank you for coming, I really appreciate it," Rodney's sister Ellen said, "his organs are shutting down, I will be turning off the machines in the morning."

Ellen lunged forward to embrace Sam.

"I'm so sorry," Sam said, stroking her hair. Ellen began sobbing into Sam's shoulder. Sam held her tight, wishing this was not her reality right now, but glad that she could help. Ellen had been through a lot, trying to take care of her small children and Rodney at the same time. Her husband had died several years earlier from a heart attack, shocking the entire community. He was in his 30's. Shortly after, Rodney started experimenting with drugs, almost killing himself several times.

Ellen had handled it all. Raising her children, making sure Rodney was cared for, mourning her husband. She always seemed to handle everything with such grace. Until today, Sam had never seen her cry. Not when Ellen had admitted Rodney into the assisted living facility, not even when Sam had called her to let her know he was on his way to the hospital.

"Did you know that when we were little, Rodney was my protector?" Ellen said between sobs.

"No, I had no idea, what was he like?" Sam asked.

"Oh, Rod was amazing. He is two years older than me and by all accounts, was protective of me from day one. He taught me how to ride a bike. He beat up the first boy who broke my heart. He held me when our parents died. He offered to take me to prom when I got stood up. He has always been my rock. And now?" Ellen started sobbing again, sobs that shook her whole body.

"I'm so sorry Ellen. He knows you love him, he always has. I know you will miss him, I'm so sorry," Sam said, holding Ellen tight.

Ellen pulled back, took a deep breath and said, "truth is, Rod has been battling demons for a long time. His battle is over. I need to let him go, no matter how much it hurts. For me to keep him, like this... it would be selfish."

"Yes. You are right, Ellen, you are right. If you need anything at all, please let me know. I will be around to talk to you anytime," Sam said.

"I will, thank you. I will be all alone here in the morning if you would like to stop in. I am sure I could use some support," Ellen said, looking into Sam's eyes.

"I will be honored to be here with you, Ellen," Sam said to her, "I will leave you for now, but I will be back in the morning."

Sam gave her a final hug and left the hospital. She fought the urge to stay, knowing that Ellen needed some time alone with Rod.

"Hey, hon, I'm on my way home, sorry I'm so late," Sam said into her cellphone.

"No problem at all, I was thinking of ordering a pizza, does that sound alright?" John replied.

"Pizza sounds fine, I don't have much of an appetite, though. I will be home soon," Sam said, hanging up the phone.

On the drive home, Sam thought about the sibling bond that Ellen and Rodney had. She had often wished that she had a big brother, or a baby sister. She couldn't fully understand the loss that Ellen felt, but if all grief was similar, she had an idea. Samantha thought of her mother, of her life since that fateful day. She wondered how different things could have been. She wondered if Jacob would still have been alive if her mother had not died.

"Sam, don't do that! You didn't cause Jacob to die, nor did it have anything to do with your mom!" she told herself, "but had Mom been here, she would have made me go to the doctor sooner," she argued in her head, "there was probably nothing that could change it. It just was. Nothing will change it now."

Sam shook her head, trying to focus on the traffic in front of her. She had been thinking about her mom a lot lately. Would her mom like John? What would she think of her paintings, the way she cooked, how she wore her hair? Would she live nearby? Would she play tennis? Would she laugh? Would she be an artist or a professional, or maybe both? Would she be loving? And yes, would Jacob be alive if her mom was here?

Sam put the car in park, looking up, startled. She didn't remember the drive. Yet here she was, in her driveway. Taking a deep breath, Sam got out of her car and went into the house. She was trying to stop all of those questions from flowing.

"Hey hon, the pizza just got here a few minutes ago, why don't you just get comfortable in the living room and I will bring you a plate," John hollered from the kitchen.

Samantha took her shoes off and plopped onto the couch. She felt like the wind was out of her sails, suddenly exhausted.

"Whoa, are you alright?" John said as he carried the plates into the room, "you don't look so good, babe."

"Oh, I'm ok, it has just been a really challenging day and tomorrow will be worse," Sam said. As they ate their pizza she told him about Ellen, and about Rodney, about how Ellen has lost so many people and now she is having to make that decision, the one that will end her brother's life.

"She is there all alone. She asked me to be there with her tomorrow when they unplug. I told her I would, I've already let my work know. Sometimes things don't happen right away, I'm fully prepared to be there as long as she needs me," Sam told him.

"It will be a long day, hon, but I'm glad you can be there for her. Why don't you take the bus in tomorrow, then after work I will come and either pick you up or join you there, and that way you won't have to fight traffic first thing in the morning," John suggested.

"That's a good idea. And if it happens that we are done early I will just take the bus home and let you know. I'm really exhausted, I hope you don't mind if I just go to bed," Sam said, standing up.

"Get your rest, sweet dreams," John said, standing to kiss her good night.

Chapter 15

Sam woke early the next morning, feeling extremely rested. She didn't remember any tossing or turning, nor did she recall waking up at all throughout the night. Samantha was grateful for the energy she felt, knowing this day was likely to leave her depleted. There were only a couple dozen people on the bus, so no one sat immediately next to her. Sam was thankful because it left her alone with her thoughts. She liked to watch people and make up stories about their lives.

Young man in jeans and a sweatshirt is on his way to meet his friends in the park to play basketball. Young woman with scarf and headphones had a fight with her parents this morning and stormed out, no real destination planned. Old man, near the front, he is a widower. He is going to the doctor because his knee has been aching.

Before she knew it, they had arrived at the hospital. She grabbed her purse and stood up to exit. However, as she did so, moving to stand up like normal, Sam fell flat on her face. Whoosh, down she went, in the middle of the bus aisle. She quickly got up, searched around to grab her bag and a few items that had fallen out. Samantha wanted to get off of the bus, she felt like everyone was staring at her. And they were.

"Are you alright young lady?" a man asked her as he helped her up.

"What happened? Are you ok?" the young girl said.

"I'm alright, thank you," Samantha stammered, "I need to go, I'm ok."

"Miss, you should get checked out, your knee looks like it's bleeding, can I walk with you to the clinic here?" the old man asked.

"No, I'm fine. I need to go, Rodney is dying, I have to go," Samantha blurted out and immediately regretted as everyone stared at her. She quickly exited the bus, not looking back. As soon as she entered the building, she went into the restroom. She looked in the mirror. Sam was a little disheveled, but not bad. She looked down at her clothes. She had chosen khaki pants today and a light blue t-shirt. Just as the old man said, her right knee was bleeding. She pulled up her pant leg and dabbed at it with a wet paper towel. Just a scrape, but it was already bruising and causing her to limp a little. The bleeding had stopped. She wet another paper towel and blotted at her pants leg, trying to make it look a little better. She looked at her watch, it was time to meet Ellen. However she looked, it had to be ok. Samantha walked quickly down to ICU.

When she got to Rodney's room, Ellen wasn't there. Sam walked over to Rodney, brushed the back of her hand on his cheek and said, "I'm glad to know you, Rodney, thank you."

"We were all lucky to have known him, Sam, thank you for being here," Ellen said, startling Sam. The doctor and a nurse came in within a few seconds. Ellen must have been signing all the papers. Sam moved back and Ellen leaned over, kissing Rodney on the cheek. She then sat next to the bed and held his hand, "I love you, Rod" she whispered.

The doctor looked at Ellen and she nodded her head. He reached over and turned the machines off one by one. The only sound in the room was the beep, beep, beeping of the ECG. Then he turned that off. And the only sound was breathing. He and the nurse walked out of the room.

Sam moved to the other side of the bed and sat in a chair, leaning forward to hold Rodney's other hand. Ellen began to sing "you are my sunshine" softly to him. Sam remembered her mom had sang that to her. She watched as Rodney's chest continued to move up and down, his breaths were slow, drawn out. Ellen choked back a sob and caressed Rodney's face.

"You know, Rod was on the chess team. Not only that, but he was the best one in our whole school. He said he could see all the moves in his head, before they happened. Everyone knew that my big brother was so smart," Ellen said.

"And most people wouldn't think that being on the chess team would make a person popular, but Rod here, he was Mr. Popular, that's for sure," Ellen continued, "girls used to call our house all the time, hoping to talk to Rod. They would call to ask for help with their homework, funny thing is, he always attracted the smart girls. They didn't need any help with their homework! Rod would always entertain their requests though and the girls often came over for tutoring. He sure knew how to capitalize on that, let me tell you! I don't think there was a single Friday night that he wasn't out on a date all during high school. Did you know..."

Ellen trailed off because Rodney skipped a breath. Then he started back up again.

"Did you know that he was a teacher? He got his teaching degree and taught history in a high school. He loved it. His wife was a teacher as well. She taught English. They were married for I think 6 years. She left him though. Ran off with someone from their church of all things. She broke his heart. That was when he started making bad choices," Ellen said.

They sat awhile in silence, each subconsciously holding their breath every time there was a pause between his breaths.

"Ellen, I'm going to go get us something to drink. Would you like anything to eat?" Sam asked.

"No, I don't think I could eat, but I am thirsty, thank you," Ellen replied, adding, "please hurry."

Sam got directions to the nearest vending machine. She got bottled water, juice, sports drinks. She had forgotten to ask Ellen what she wanted, so she grabbed a couple of each. She rushed back to the room and found Ellen singing to Rod again. Sam noticed that his breaths were further apart, that his chest isn't moving as much. She sat some drinks on the side table near Ellen and went back to her chair. Ellen paused to get a drink, just as they heard a gurgling sound coming from Rodney.

"Is he in pain?" Ellen asked her, sounding panicked.

"No, this is normal. His breathing is slowing, his body will make some sounds, he probably won't be with us much longer, I'm sorry," Sam answered.

"How do you know so much about all of this?" Ellen asked her.

"I have worked with hospice quite a bit. I have always thought it was such an honor to be present in someone's last moments. You might think that's morbid, but I think it is amazing to honor them by helping them to transition peacefully," Sam responded

"I think that's beautiful, thank you," Ellen said, then she looked at Rod, "it's ok, big brother, I will be alright. I want you to find your peace."

With a slow exhalation, Rod was gone. Ellen closed her eyes and began sobbing. Sam moved over to put her arms around Ellen, she held onto her as she cried. Sam knew that in this moment, Ellen just needed to be held. She needed to have someone there to support her. There were no words necessary. She had no idea how much time had passed, but the nurse walked by, noticed what was going on and called the doctor in.

"We are sorry for your loss, Ellen," the doctor said.

"Thank you," she said, barely discernable through her sobs.

"Take your time here, and please let us know if you need anything," the doctor said, "please just let us know before you leave, if you would."

Ellen took a deep breath, leaned over and kissed Rodney on the cheek, let out a small sob and turned to Samantha, "thank you so much for spending this day with me. I need to get away, to breathe some fresh air, to see my children now. I can't be here any more."

"Thank you for allowing me to be with you. Will you be alright to drive home?" Sam responded.

"Oh yes, I will be alright, and I will stop in to let you all know when the services will be, thank you again," Ellen said, hugging Sam tightly.

Sam left the room and headed towards an exit. Fresh air does indeed sound nice right now. She got out her phone to text John, she figured she would just ride the bus home, but instead she found a text from him saying he was on his way. She sat down in the grass and waited. As she did so, her knee ached and she remembered this morning, then she noticed the stain on her pants. John will notice that right away. She realized that there was nothing she could do about it now. Samantha also realized that she had no energy to come up with a believable story either. She sighed, it has been a long day.

Chapter 16

"Hey there, sweetheart, how are you?" John said as he approached, "what happened to your knee?"

"Oh, I tripped on the bus this morning. No big deal. A scrape and a bruise. You have good timing, Rodney died about a half hour ago," Samantha said.

"I'm sorry, hon, are you alright?" John said, hugging her.

"Yeah, I'm fine. I knew what would happen before I got here. Ellen has been talking through everything all day, I think she has been processing, and that's good," Sam replied.

"It doesn't bother you, Sam? When someone dies?" John asked.

"Everyone dies, John. It bothers me, when people go needlessly, but there is a natural order to things. I'm so honored to be able to hold that space for them as they transition. Not only that though, but to be there to be a calm force for the family. To be the strength and support that they need, being the example for them, does that make sense," Sam asked.

"It does, Sam, and you are a remarkable woman. I just want to make sure that you are ok, and I will doctor up your knee when we get home," John said.

"Yes, doctor John," Sam said, rolling her eyes at him, "oh, hey, I haven't eaten today, I'm starving."

"Well, let's get some food in you first. Would you like to go out somewhere? Or would you like me to make you something at home?" he asked her.

"Can we go to the market and see what they have in the deli? Then just take it home to eat? That sounds more relaxing than going out somewhere," Sam suggested.

In the market, Sam headed to the salad bar. She loved this salad bar, it always had exactly what she wanted. John got a pot pie, Sam got her salad, and they looked for drinks but decided on the wine they had at home.

After dinner, Sam sat back on the couch, shutting her eyes.

"I know it's been a long day, babe, but I need to look at your knee, I need you out of those pants," John said.

Sam took her pants off and sat on the couch so John could look at her knee. He brought the first aid kit and sat on the coffee table to get a better look. He cleaned it with a wet cloth and poured some peroxide on it.

"The scrape isn't so bad, but the bruising looks terrible. Does it hurt when you bend it like this?" he asked as he bent her leg.

Sam winced in pain as she answered, "yeah, it hurts, but it's just bruised. Plus I should have iced it earlier, but It just wasn't my top priority, you know?"

"I understand, Sam, I just worry about you. You should be on the mend now though," he said as he put a bandage on her knee.

"Thanks hon for taking such good care of me, I really appreciate it. And I know I went to bed early last night, but I'm exhausted and I need some rest." Sam said to John.

"I will be up in a few minutes, I am pretty tired this evening as well. Sweet dreams," John said as Sam headed to bed.

Chapter 17

"Sandra, can I talk to you for a minute?" Samantha asked the nurse the next morning at work.

"Sure, anytime, what can I do for you, Sam?" Sandra replied.

"Well, you know the difficulties I've been having. I fell down my stairs, got dizzy and lost my balance," Sam began, "well, yesterday, I rode the bus to the hospital to be with Ellen, and when we got there, I stood up, but it's like my legs weren't even under me. I fell flat on my face. Not really on my face, but I did go down, and hard. I quickly recovered but it was the strangest thing. When I got up, my legs were working fine, though a bit bruised and bloody."

"Sam, you must make an appointment. Your doctor will likely refer you to a neurologist who will run some basic tests and likely order an MRI. The MRI will be the method of choice because that's the best test to determine if someone has MS. I'm not saying you do, but with your family history, they would want to rule that out. Your health isn't anything to mess around with. Whatever is causing this, well, I'm sure there's an explanation and treatment for it," Sandra said.

"I will call my doctor today and make an appointment. I have to tell you though, that it is scary. I wonder sometimes if I want to know the answer here. If I am diagnosed with something, and find out it's not just a fluke, then there will be no going back," Sam replied.

"It will be better to know and treat it, than to just let things run their course," Sandra said as Sam got up to leave.

"I'm not so sure," Sam thought to herself.

The rest of the day at work, between testing blood sugars, giving showers, helping residents with daily tasks, Sam was lost in a place she called "What If Land." What if she had MS. What if it was a tumor. What if she had cancer. What if she was dying. A bit morbid, perhaps, but Sam liked to consider all possibilities, and maybe drive herself a little insane at the same time. She called and made an appointment for the following week, but had already decided to not speak to John about it.

Sam remembered when her mom was diagnosed with MS. Her husband left her the day she received her diagnosis. She had stood by his side through a cancer diagnosis and treatment, heart attacks, but when she was diagnosed, he was gone. Not that she thought for a moment that John would do that. Samantha thought about her early life, taking care of her mom. She could never ask all of that of John. She shook her head, realizing she was way ahead of the game here. She hadn't received any sort of diagnosis yet and all of the things going on with her could be unrelated.

She wasn't even sure what she should tell her doctor. One time, she fell on the bus, a few days before, she fell down the stairs, and she had gotten dizzy. All of a sudden, she felt like she was making way too much of this. These were three basically harmless instances. However, the appointment was already made. She would just tell her doctor that a few things have been happening, perhaps an ear infection, or vertigo. No big deal. Of course, she didn't recall being dizzy on the bus. At any rate, she had no time for illness right now. It simply was not convenient. She laughed at the ridiculousness of that thought. Sam doubted that her mom had felt her illness was timed well.

"Sam, do you have a minute?" Sandra asked.

"Of course, what's going on?" Sam replied.

"I need you to come into the med room with me," Sandra asked.

Sam felt uneasy. Sandra looked quite serious and Sam felt like she was in some kind of trouble. She thought about the morning's routine. She gave the meds, watched the residents swallow them, tested blood sugars, administered insulin, wrote in the charts…. she couldn't think of a single thing she had missed.

"I was going over the records and Mr. Williams' narcotic count is off. There seems to be one that isn't signed out for, and you know as well as I do how serious this is," Sandra said to her once they were alone in the room.

"Oh, Bob had come in, he said his back was hurting him terribly, I saw that he could have a Darvocet, let me see his records," Samantha said, thumbing through the med book, "oh yes, see, I gave him a Darvocet this morning."

"It isn't signed out in the narcotics book. Please fill it in properly. I see what happened, but you know that we have to be extremely cautious with narcotics, well, with all the meds, but we are under the most scrutiny with controlled drugs. Sam, this isn't like you. If this continues to happen, you will have to be taken off meds," Sandra said. "Also, it is time to follow up and note whether the medication helped his pain or not. Sam, are you alright to be doing this job today? I need you to be present."

"I'm sorry, Sandra. I guess my mind was wandering with all of the what if's of this impending doctor's appointment. As a rule, I'm 100% here, but today I just seem to be drifting. I just keep thinking about my mom and her diagnosis, about how many years she had after that diagnosis, and the lack of quality in those years. I just feel lost," Sam said.

"I'll tell you what, Sam, you go check with Bob and log whether the medication helped him and then I'll take over for you for the day, I'll give the meds at lunch. You go home and rest, I will let Jack know that I sent you home," Sandra replied.

"Thank you Sandra, I promise I will get my head screwed on right. I will come back fully present. Thank you for understanding," Sam said, "I'll go check with Bob and then I'll go after I make the notes."

Samantha walked down the hallway to Bob's room. He didn't answer immediately when she knocked and that worried her. She used her key to enter.

"Bob, are you here?" Sam asked, entering the room. She found Bob napping on his bed, she quietly asked "how is your back feeling? Did the Darvocet help?"

"Oh yes, much better sweetie, it helped," he replied, then rolled over.

Sam went into the med room and made all the necessary notations in Bob's book, counted narcotics with Sandra and signed the med key over to her.

"Thank you, Sandra. I will see you tomorrow," Sam said as she left the room.

On her drive home, she was thinking about the doctor's appointment. It was probably unnecessary, Sam decided. Every single thing that happened could be explained away. She tripped on the stairs, she had vertigo, and on the bus... well, she didn't really have a reason for that. She had to admit that together all of these things were concerning. Separate, they were benign, but together, a little scary.

Chapter 18

When she got home, Sam decided she would take a nap. She has been tired lately, and assumed that was due to her work schedule. It was warm today, so she turned on the box fan on her side of the bed. John had put one on each side the other night to help keep them cool. As she drifted off to sleep she realized she hadn't painted in over a week.

Sam woke with a feeling of urgency. She felt panicked, like she had to be somewhere and overslept. She jumped up out of bed. She started sprinting towards the door, but had no feelings in her legs. Down she went, crashing into the box fan, cutting her leg open.

"Dammit!" Sam yelled as she looked at her knee. The cut was too deep for a bandage, but she felt like she could bandage it enough to drive herself to the clinic. The bedroom was a bit of a mess, but that would have to wait. Sam pressed a gauze pad on the wound and then wrapped with an ace bandage. She did her best to ignore the pain radiating from the cut.

The drive to the clinic was uneventful, but when she arrived, she noticed that her wound was bleeding quite a bit. The intake nurse took all of Sam's information and told her that she would be called back shortly. Sam knew that any number of cases would be more important than her getting a few stitches, so she planned to wait awhile. She looked at her watch. At least three more hours until John gets home. If all went well, she would be home before him.

She realized that she wouldn't be able to hide this from him. It's just a cut on her leg though. He would just have to think that she forgot about the fan being there and tripped over it. Likely he would think she is getting rather clumsy lately, but

Samantha doubted he would think much more of it. Unfortunately, she wouldn't be able to go in the hot tub for a while.

Her leg had started throbbing and she was bleeding through the ace bandage. She looked up to see a man hobbling in, supporting himself on a woman's shoulder. They quickly grabbed a wheelchair for him. She overheard the couple talking to the intake nurse. Apparently the man had run over his foot with the lawn mower. He had been wearing flip-flops, and they had his big toe in a bag with a bag of peas. They rushed him back.

There was another man rushed in via ambulance. Heart attack, they said as they rushed him in. Samantha was not religious, but found herself saying a prayer for the doctors involved in the care of these men. She looked around the waiting room. There were several children who seemed to be having the severe cold that was going around. The woman who came in with the man who was having the heart attack was crying between conversations on her cell phone.

Samantha considering going over and trying to comfort her, but the woman was quickly joined by two men. She watched how they interacted, and looked closely at the three of them. The men must be in their early twenties, and twins. Samantha also decided they were the couple's sons. They seemed to be very protective of their mother, and slightly distraught at the circumstances. The sons each were texting others as well, and Sam assumed that they were each keeping friends and family apprised of what was going on.

Her thoughts drifted to her own mother. Sam wondered if her mom had ever gone through anything like what this woman is going through. She also wondered if she would be there to support her like these boys were doing with their mother. She wondered if her mother would approve of her choices in life. Samantha was sure that her mom would love John. Everyone loved John. Everything came so easy to him, it seemed. Well, except for the perfect wife and two children that he had dreamed of, she thought bitterly.

Samantha was surprised at her feelings when she thought of John. She wondered where this animosity came from. As a general rule, she thought of John with nothing but love and admiration. He was a hard worker, had great relationships with his family members. John was always kind, would never harm a soul. Lately, though, well, since she became pregnant with Jacob, John has been different. He has been treating her like she needs protecting. John had changed from being the loving husband to placing her up on a pedestal. Sam didn't want to be a prized object, a protected person. She wanted to be a loving, and much loved wife.

Of course, part of the reason Sam felt this way was because she had lost Jacob, she couldn't make John's dreams come true. She couldn't even give him the son he so badly wanted, the son he so badly deserved. That, and the fact that she simply couldn't be the lovey dovey wife that he needed. She couldn't fawn over him at company parties like he deserved. She was socially inept, not the wife he deserved.

"Samantha?" the nurse called.

Sam hopped up, immediately regretting that decision, nearly fell over from pain in her leg and said "coming" quite weakly in response.

"What happened to your leg?" the doctor said, removing her bandages, "oh my, that's a nasty cut."

"I got up from a nap and tripped over a box fan," Sam answered calmly, "can I lay back, please, I'm feeling a little weak."

"Of course, lay back, I am going to have my nurse clean it up but first I'm going to give you some shots to help it not hurt so bad. I think about 4 shots around the wound should do it. You will feel a little poke each time, but then the pain should ease up, ok? I'm all done, actually, should have warned you before I did it but I find that it works out better if I don't."

Sam closed her eyes while the nurse cleaned out the wound. She felt a tugging and a pressure on her leg, but it didn't hurt. The nurse made small talk while she performed her tasks. She may have asked Samantha some questions, but Sam was not altogether sure that she had answered. When Sam opened her eyes, the doctor was back in the room and the nurse was getting all of his equipment ready.

"It looks like you will be needing some stitches, and your leg is going to hurt for some time. No baths or swimming until the stitches are out, and no showers for a couple days. The stitches should be out in about two weeks and you will be left with a scar. I will send you home with a prescription for pain pills. You will need to keep the area clean and dry, and change your bandage once a day for the first few days, after that it will be fine to leave the bandage off, of course, with it being right above your knee, the more you wear shorts and let it air out, the better. You should have normal range of motion, and if there are any problems, please see your doctor right away," the doctor said as he worked, "you are good as new, young lady, take care of yourself and no more wrestling with box fans, alright?" the doctor laughed as he finished writing in the chart.

Chapter 19

Samantha looked at her watch. She would definitely not beat John home, especially if she was going to get her prescription filled. She decided a preemptive call was in order.

"Hey hon, I will be a few minutes late, would you like me to grab dinner on my way? Oh, you are cooking already? Great, well I won't be long," Sam said into her phone and hung up.

Sam was relieved to find there was no line at the pharmacy. She was in and out quickly and when she got home, John was finishing with dinner preparations. He stopped to kiss her and noticed her knee. "What happened, Sam?"

"Oh, well, I took a nap and when I got up I tripped over the box fan. I broke it and a shard of the plastic got embedded in my leg. So, I pulled it out, wrapped it up and got some stitches. I should be good as new within a couple weeks! What's for dinner?" Samantha spoke quickly, hoping to brush over the whole event.

"Wow, hon, why didn't you call me so that I could take you to the emergency room?" John said, looking quite hurt.

"I'm sorry John, honestly, I just went into that mode and set out to fix the problem. I didn't want to worry you, and I didn't feel like it was a big deal. My life was never in danger, just a cut and a few stitches. Please don't be angry with me," Samantha pleaded.

"I'm not angry, you know I worry, and if you are going to just take charge and not let me help, that is a bit bothersome to me, but I'm not angry," John said, sounding defeated.

"Oh John, I just didn't want to bother you, I didn't want you to worry, and I didn't want you to have to save me. I think you always have to save me, and that is going to get old to you," Samantha explained.

"What are you talking about?" John was practically yelling at this point, "I am your husband, it is my job to take care of you, to keep you safe, to nurse you when you are ill! It is not something that will get old, it will never get old!"

"I'm sorry, John, I wasn't thinking," Samantha whispered.

They ate in silence, Sam knew that true to form, John was trying to figure out how to fix this, how to mold her into the perfect wife. She felt bad for not being a better wife. She had always known that she couldn't be who he needed. She didn't know how to be a good wife, would likely never find out if she had the ability to be a good mother. Especially with all of these odd things going on, with wondering if there is something medically wrong with her. That thought startled her. What if John knew all of the things going on with her? What if he started to connect the dots? He would never forgive her, that's for sure. Samantha sighed, then he can never know.

"What's wrong? Does your leg hurt?" John asked.

Even though it wasn't bothering her, it was the perfect out, Samantha realized.

"Yes, it is throbbing. I think I should take one of my pain pills, but that's likely to put me to sleep," Sam replied.

"Well, let me get you to bed then," John replied, while holding out his hand to her. He helped her upstairs to bed and tucked her in, "I do love you Sam, you know that, right?"

"Of course I do," Sam said sleepily and closed her eyes.

Sam's dreams were thick with monsters, lava, and doom. She was running from a dragon who was shooting fire at her, then found herself on a cliff, looking over a sea of lava. Nowhere to go, and her screams caught in her throat as the dragon approached. However, it fell dead at her feet, having been slayed by a handsome prince that she can now see. The prince trips as he is running to her and falls into the lava.

Sam bolted upright in her sleep, letting out a mere whimper.

"Are you alright, Sammi?" John said, "what's wrong?"

"Oh, I'm ok, was just having weird dreams. I don't think I will be taking the pain pills anymore," Sam said.

"Sam, that's just like you. The pain pills were prescribed to help you deal with the pain. You can't just arbitrarily decide to stop taking them," John lectured, sounding annoyed.

"I will be fine, John. I don't need narcotics to deal with a few stitches," Samantha replied, with finality. They each rolled over, facing away from the other, and went to sleep.

By morning, Sam's leg was throbbing. She wanted nothing more than to take a hot bath until she felt better. Baths were always her way of soothing herself. Not having that option, though, Sam decided that a walk around the house would likely help. Pain shot up her leg as soon as she put weight on it. Samantha pushed through and walked around the entire house, including down the stairs. Of course, the stairs were taken a little slower than she would have liked. After her morning's exercise, she decided to take some acetaminophen.

Sam was starting to doubt her decision to stop taking the pain pills. Her leg was throbbing. She knew that she had overdone it. Yet, her stubbornness kept her from admitting that she was wrong. Samantha was glad that today was a day off. Pain to Samantha was a sleep serum. If she was in pain, then exhaustion was not far behind. Sam laid down on the couch to look at a magazine. She woke up several hours later, her leg throbbing, and stunned at the passing of time. She still had several hours before John was due home but she had been hoping to paint today. She hopped up, forgetting about the pain until it shot through her body, momentarily sat down, then got back up again.

She chose a canvas, and started with red, orange, and black. Samantha began painting the canvas, layering the colors on, blending, swirling, covering. Once the canvas was covered she stepped back and gasped. She had just painted the lava from her dream. She decided to leave it on the easel to dry, that way she would be able to look at it and see if she could figure it out over the next few days. Why was there lava in her dream? Why did the prince fall into the lava as soon as he saved her? Was it a prophecy about her life? Was John there to save her? And would that act bring him to his impending death? Has she already ruined his life, Samantha wondered. Samantha let her mind wander to all of the things that have been happening to her, health-wise. The vertigo, the falling, forgetting to chart properly at work. She wondered what was going on. She had never been this clumsy before, nor had she been this scared, she realized.

Chapter 20

"So what brings you here today, Sam? I see that you fell yesterday? How many stitches did you get?" Dr. Burke asked her.

"I got 8, but today's visit isn't about that, well, not totally," Sam replied, "there have been some things going on with me lately and I just wanted to talk to you about them."

Dr. Burke looked concerned, "alright, let's get started. Tell me what's been going on, when it started, all of it."

Sam told her about falling down the stairs, about hearing the metallic sound prior to her vertigo, about falling in the bus because of a complete lack of feeling in her legs, and how that happened again on the box fan. She also told her about being forgetful at work.

"And all of this has happened in the past... three weeks?" the doctor asked.

"Yes, at first, I thought nothing of it, but then things kept piling up. And with my family history, I felt like it was better to rule out any problems," Samantha replied, stressing "rule out".

Dr. Burke thumbed through Samantha's chart, "oh yes, your mother had Multiple sclerosis. I can see how these things are concerning for you. Let's not jump to any conclusions though, alright? I will run a series of neurological tests and will likely order an MRI. If all is inconclusive, we may decide to do a spinal tap as a final test."

And just like that, the battery of appointments began. John went out of town for a work conference, thankfully, so she didn't have to account for all the time these appointments took. Blood Work, MRI, follow up appointments with Dr. Burke after each test. Every test she ran on Sam's blood work was within normal limits, so that ruled out blood sugar issues, infections, even cancer.

Sam hated lying in the metal tube for the MRI. She despised the metal cage around her head, disliked being confined and having to hold still. Every time she was told by someone that she couldn't move, something would itch, or she would feel a sneeze coming on. She remembered being in choir in junior high, she would feel perfectly fine, then the curtain would go up and she would see the audience and her nose would itch like mad. Choir concerts had nothing on an MRI machine, though, and Sam was thankful when she was done.

Unfortunately, she wouldn't have the results from this until after John returned from his trip. She will just have to schedule the appointment while he is at work. She will make her decisions after that. She had been thinking about John. She loved John deeply, but there was no way she was going to put him through having to take care of her as she died. She had been through that with her mom. She remembered her step-dad's reaction when he found out her mom had MS. He bolted, never to be heard from again. John would never have that reaction, he would stay until the bitter end, tube feeding her, wiping her butt, no thank you. As far as Samantha was concerned, there was only one option, and that was to cut John loose if she is ill. Since John is the man he is, the man that she fell in love with, she could not tell him about her illness. He would never let her leave if she did.

Samantha would have to figure out how to end this. She could have an affair. She could become violent. Sam didn't like either of those options. If only she could walk away, yet give him closure, without breaking his heart. Talk about reaching for the impossible! She let her mind drift... what if she stayed with John. What if they are meant to be together forever? Then she imagined, what if he could get a caregiver for her, so the daily care things could be managed by someone else. No. He would still see her wasting away before his eyes. Her initial decision is the one she would stick with. If she finds out that she is terminally ill, then she will find a way to end her marriage.

The remainder of the days that John was on his trip crawled by. Sam was thankful to be kept busy at work and had been doing a good job of crossing her t's and dotting her i's to stay under the radar with Sandra. However, Sandra had noticed her limping on her first day back. Samantha had no choice but to tell her about the incident with the box fan. Sandra looked very concerned, but Sam cut her off, "The doctor knows about everything that's been going on and he is running tests."

"Ok, good, I worry, you know," Sandra replied.

"I know, I do too, to be honest. You know, when my mom was diagnosed, her husband was out the door. Practically before she could finish the sentence," Samantha told her.

"Oh you know John isn't like that!" Sandra said. She had been to John and Sam's for dinner, and was the only one who visited them immediately after Jacob's birth.

"Can I talk to you for a minute, Sandra?" Sam asked her, when Sandra nodded, she continued, "I know that John loves me. But I've been the caregiver for someone with MS, for my mom. It is the most difficult, most horrible thing to go through, especially when it's a role that is just thrown at you. I won't do that to John. He would never leave me, I know that. But if I get this diagnosis, I have to find a way to cut him loose."

Sandra looked at her, "Sam, that choice isn't yours to make."

"Yeah, it is. It is only mine, and I won't do that to him," Sam said with finality as she walked towards the door.

Samantha wondered if it was wise to talk with Sandra about it, but she was glad she had done it. She could feel her resolve strengthen. Of course, what she was hoping for most was to find out that there was nothing medically wrong with her. She couldn't shake the feeling that was a false hope, though. Samantha shook her head, it wasn't like her to be so pessimistic.

Chapter 21

A vision came into her head, her mother's funeral. Beautiful white casket with pale pink roses, her mom in a dress she had picked, she looked like an angel. It was the first funeral that Samantha had ever been to. She found it strange how the family sat off to the side, so segregated.

The placement made it clear how different they were, those in that group, from anyone else there. Their loss was more real, and they were tainted with grief. Samantha remembered feeling distanced from everything that happened during that time, like she was merely an observer. School was like that afterwards too, she observed, she held back, she was there, but not a part of.

Sam began to wonder if she had merely been observing her whole life. If she is sick, if she is dying, will anyone remember her? In fact, whether she has MS or not, when she dies, will it matter to anyone? She supposed that if she was still married to John that he would care. But had she impacted anyone else? Or would hers be that moss covered headstone that never has a single visitor? Samantha sighed, so many questions, including this one: is Samantha Green worth saving?

Sam realized there was nothing in color in her life. She lived in shades of grey. She was good with the residents, but she was also very clinical. They didn't consider her family, or even a friend. Samantha was their caregiver. She wasn't active in any church or community groups, she didn't volunteer anywhere, had never shown her paintings, been on tv or radio. She couldn't even give birth to a baby to bring color to her world. Sam sighed and tried to focus on work. John would be home tonight, she realized with a sigh.

She missed John, she realized, but if she had to set him free, how would a romantic reunion help? She realized she was creating more problems than she was solving since she had no MRI results yet, but she simply couldn't lead him on if there was any possibility of being diagnosed with anything terminal.

"What a tangled web we weave, when we practice to deceive," she quoted to herself. For a brief moment, she thought she could just live happily ever after, then the memory of her mom in a casket flashed into her mind. No. She would not have John be the broken husband at a funeral, with no friends to support him because he had devoted his entire life to her. She needed to formulate a plan. Samantha actually found herself wishing that she had a bad head cold, or the flu, then he would understand her not cuddling up to him. However, she didn't even have a sniffle. She looked at her watch, less that 4 hours to figure it out.

After work, Sam knew she had some time to kill and was nervous, so she went to a local Mexican restaurant to get some food and devise a plan. Samantha ate a soft taco and had some nachos while jotting down some ideas. She felt like a criminal, and had to keep reminding herself that it's not like she was hiring a hitman or something. She was leaving everyone alive, well, John, and was making decisions based on his well being. Sam was only doing what needed to be done in order for John to be happy in life. At least, that's what she told herself.

Before Sam got home, her stomach started gurgling. She didn't feel very well, and she feared there was something wrong with her dinner. She rushed into the house, tossing her purse in the entryway on her way in. She barely made it to the restroom on time.

"Are you ok, hon?" John said through the bathroom door.

"Yeah, I'm sorry, I'm so sick, going to be in here awhile," Samantha responded.

"Just make sure to give me a yell if you need anything, ok, hon?" John said.

"Ok, thanks. Welcome home, sorry," Sam replied.

When Samantha finally got to bed, John was sound asleep. Sam was grateful to not have to worry about small talk tonight. As she drifted off to sleep, she remembered that John was going golfing in the morning, so tomorrow should be easy enough to get through. They would likely only be around one another at dinner. Sam figured that she could do that. It wasn't like she hated him, she just didn't want to hurt him any more than she needed to. Her last thought as she was falling asleep was: why couldn't it have been a virus or the flu? Something that lasted more than one day.

Sam heard John rustling around the next morning, and though she was wide awake, she pretended to be asleep. John kissed her on the cheek prior to going golfing. Only after she heard the garage door close did Samantha open her eyes and think about getting out of bed. She needed to figure out a way to spend her day. A productive way that would occupy her mind in addition to her time. She considered painting, but when she went to paint, she was faced with that damned lava painting. Samantha shook her head and walked away. She didn't feel like she could face that today. After ruling out painting, Sam walked around the house, wondering what she could do.

She got caught up on laundry, she mopped the floors, she even shampooed the carpets in the living room before John got home.

"Wow, you've been busy," John said when he got home. He walked over to her and kissed her cheek, "how are you feeling?"

"I'm feeling so much better," Sam said, "my stomach is still not great, but at least I'm upright today and can function. How was your trip?"

"Oh it was good. The usual work conference," John replied, "it was nice not having to go alone this time. Always better to be in an unfamiliar city with a friendly face."

"I didn't know anyone else from the firm went with you. Who went? Ken?" Samantha inquired.

"Oh, I thought I told you. Renee went with me," John said, and only Sam would have noticed his color change when he did so. She knew him better than anyone else, yet this news was startling to her.

"Your assistant? How did that come about? I thought the company was going through some budget cuts," Sam asked.

"Um, well, they are," John stammered, "I guess they figured I would retain more if I had an extra set of eyes and ears there."

"That's interesting. Did it help? Did you learn more?," Samantha asked, pondering for the first time since she met John that he could be unfaithful to her. She wanted to scream, to cry, to throw something at him. Yet, wasn't this what she was looking for? A reason to end her marriage?

"I'm not sure, I think it helped, but like I said, it made the week go by better since I knew someone there," John said, "are you up to eating, hon?"

"You know, my stomach is really bothering me, and I should probably lie down. If you want some company though, Renee might be free," Samantha responded. As soon as the words were out of her mouth, she regretted them. She didn't even know that John and Renee had done anything. She realized, that since this may help her to end her marriage, and she was seizing it like a dog with a steak, that she was acting like an opportunistic bitch.

"Hon, I don't know where you are coming from, here. I thought I had told you that Renee was going on this conference with me. She helped with notes, actually recorded each class and typed up notes for me, also she was invaluable when it came time for me to teach my class. I don't know what I would have done without her," John said.

"Great, like I said, maybe she is available for dinner," Sam spat at him.

"You know, that's a great idea, I need to thank her for all she did for me anyway," John said, then went to take a shower. Sam heard him on his cellphone in the bathroom. When he got out, he got dressed and grabbed his keys. He didn't say a word on his way out.

When she heard the garage door close, she wept. She was surprised at his strong reaction, but she had never accused him of being unfaithful before. Samantha felt bad that it had hurt his feelings, yet, the way he responded made her seriously doubt his fidelity. Sam wondered, was this it? All of her plotting, and she is given this out? She had been wondering how to do this without breaking his heart, and it was a seemingly simple solution: her heart should break instead.

When Sam woke, she was alone in bed. She got up and found John asleep, fully clothed, on the couch. He looked like he had just passed out there, he wasn't covered up, one of his shoes was still on. It was inconceivable to her that he drove drunk so she looked out the window. His car was not in the driveway. Samantha walked over to John and tried to wake him, shaking his shoulder, but he would not rouse. She would just have to wait to get answers.

Chapter 22

Sam decided to dive into painting. When she did so, generally, time would pass quickly, she was hoping for a good distraction. She looked at the lava painting and set it aside. Sam got a new applied gesso to a canvas out and started covering it with royal blue, and orange, and then some white. She continued layering color on top of color, brushing it on, slapping some on with her paint knife, until she had a glorious sunset. She stepped back to look at it. Samantha definitely liked what she saw.

"Wow, I think that's the best one you've painted so far," John said from the doorway.

"Where's your car?" Sam asked.

"Oh, um, I think it may still be at the restaurant," John stammered.

"Did you take a cab home?" Sam asked him.

"Yes," John replied.

"How about you tell me what happened last night? We're not getting anywhere with twenty questions, and it's just going to make us both angry to piecemeal the information," Sam suggested.

"Alright, but I doubt there will be less anger this way," John said, "but yesterday you basically accused me of having an affair with Renee, and said I should take her out. You were being a bitch, frankly, and I decided that if I'm going to be accused of something, I may as well do it."

Tears began streaming down Samantha's face and she made no move to wipe them away, she just listened as John continued.

"So I got ahold of Renee, and took her out to a nice restaurant. She has hit on me a few times, and in all honesty, we have flirted, bit it was all harmless. Last night, though, as we were eating dinner, I felt her foot on my leg, moving up, and I got really nervous. I ordered another drink, and then another. I didn't know if I could have meaningless sex, but I was sure trying to work up the courage," John said. Samantha slumped down, sitting on the floor where she had been standing. I

"After a few drinks, I was a little more brave, and I started complimenting her, and reached across the table to hold her hand. She had been drinking as well, and I could tell her breathing changed as soon as I touched her. Knowing that she wanted me seemed to fuel the fire. She suggested we find a more cozy place to be, and I said 'ok, Sam, let me get the check'. Renee burst into tears and left while I fumbled to pay for the meal," John said.

Samantha just looked at him, trying to take it all in, she drew her breath in, to speak, but John began speaking again.

"I got into a cab, and the next thing I knew, I was arriving at her house, I wasn't even sure how I got there," John continued, "I knocked on her door, she answered, pretty shocked that I was there. I asked if I could come in, she moved to the side and I did. I sat on the couch and motioned for her to sit next to me, and we talked. For hours. I felt so, connected to her."

Sam sobbed, slumped down on the floor, with her back against the wall, looking only at her own feet.

"I knew I would want to be out of the house today, so I called a cab to bring me home instead of to the car. The thing is, Sam, I've realized lately that since Jacob…. well, even since you were first pregnant, I had lost you. You have been unreachable, no matter how I try. Once in awhile, I get a small glimmer of the Sam that I know is in there, but I have been lonely. I lost my best friend when you got pregnant, and when

Jacob died, I needed you, I know you needed me, but you just slipped away. I tried holding on, I have been trying so hard, and I'm lonely, and I'm exhausted," John said, tears rolling down his face.

"I'm sorry, John," Samantha whispered.

"So am I, Sammi, so am I. I'm going to go now. I can't keep doing this. I deserve to be happy, and to find someone in my life who will at least be able to open up to me. You deserve to be happy too, Sam. Maybe seeing me everyday, after going through so much, maybe if you don't have to do that, then you can finally let some happiness in," John said.

Sam didn't respond, she just sat there and cried. John walked out of the room and called a cab so he could get his car. Samantha didn't know what to do with herself. She decided that she should find out if there are any apartments for rent. She didn't want the house, nor could she afford the payments on it, with her salary. John could afford the payments, she wondered if he would keep it. John was very practical, so she doubted he would. The payments would take a big chunk of his salary and it would be a lot of space for just him. That is, if it was going to be just him. Samantha shook her head, dismissing that thought. It was none of her business who he spent his time with, and she did want him to be less lonely.

"Oh Samantha, stop acting like you have a say in this," she told herself.

In a moment of clarity, she realized that it was done. John would not be the destroyed husband at the funeral. He wouldn't have to see her deteriorate. In fact, now she had no one to mourn her. That fact made her feel both triumphant and empty. At least John would be spared, Sam thought.

The next week was a blur. Sam found an apartment, John helped her move some things into it. The bed out of the guest bedroom, some of the dishes, some cookware, towels, linens, some of the food out of the pantry, a chair and the loveseat from the living room, all of her painting supplies. She noticed that he looked tired, and she noted that he had already removed his wedding ring. Sam still wore hers. She packed her clothes in suitcases, letting him know that if he needed them back, he could have them. John just shook his head.

Chapter 23

By the time Samantha had to go to her appointment, everything was fully unpacked. Her paintings were hanging on the walls, she had bought some lamps and filled the fridge. She felt like life was beginning, in a way. Not in a shiny, new, exciting way, rather in a way that whatever her reality is now started when she moved out. She waited nervously in Dr. Burke's waiting room.

"Samantha Green?" the receptionist called.

Sam followed the nurse back to the exam room, setting her purse down so the nurse could weigh her and take her vitals. She had lost a considerable amount of weight from her last visit and the nurse insisted on re-weighing her. She looked perplexed as she wrote the number down.

"The doctor will be right with you," the nurse said, exiting the room and closing the door.

Sam didn't like this wait. At least in the waiting room, there were others there. In here, you had no choice but to be completely alone with your thoughts. Samantha sighed. It seemed like her life was made up of being alone with her thoughts. Especially now, where if she wasn't working, she may not even leave her apartment. Thankfully the residents were talkative, because Sam wasn't really friends with any of her coworkers. Katie, who had taken Samantha to painting class, had moved and no longer worked there. Her other coworkers whispered behind her back about how cold and clinical she was.

There was a light knock on the door, then Dr. Burke opened the door and came in.

"Hey, Sam, how are you feeling?" the doctor asked.

"I'm feeling alright, I haven't fallen since I saw you last, have only had a couple episodes of vertigo," Sam said.

"I noticed you have lost quite a bit of weight since you were here last. I'm quite concerned about that. What is going on?" Dr. Burke replied.

"Well, I would contribute that mostly to stress, I think. My marriage ended abruptly, I'm in a new apartment, I don't always remember to eat," Sam said.

"Oh, I'm so sorry to hear that. Divorce is a terrible stressor. I'm going to give you a chart to put on your fridge so that you remember to eat, alright? You need to give your body fuel. So, no more falls, but some vertigo. Have you had any more loss of sensation in your legs? Any tingling?" Dr. Burke asked.

"Well, no loss of sensation, but yes, some tingling in my arms and legs," Samantha admitted.

Dr. Burked thumbed through Sam's chart. Samantha wanted nothing more than to ask her what the test results were, but she didn't want to rush her, she didn't want to rush the information.

"I have your test results, as you know, all your bloodwork was normal. What that means is this isn't a blood sugar issue, your thyroid is fine, and your white blood cells are normal, so the likelihood of cancer is very slim," Dr. Burke informed her.

"Ok, that's all good news," Samantha responded, "and the MRI?"

"Yes, the MRI. Let me show you some films from that," Dr. Burke replied, as she got up, put some films up on the light wall, and dimmed the lights a little, "this is your brain, obviously. These white spots you see? There are five of them... those are not there on a healthy brain. Those lesions are indicative of Multiple sclerosis. You are familiar with the things that go on in your brain when you have MS, from your childhood."

Dr. Burke sat next to Samantha. She reached over and put her hand on top of Sam's, "I'm sorry, Samantha. You have multiple sclerosis, and I believe the kind you have is relapsing-remitting, though time will tell that a bit better. What that means is that you will get worse, then you'll get some better, then you'll worsen, get a bit better, etc. There are some treatments, to slow the progression and I would like to get started on those right away. I know this is a lot to take in, but the sooner we start treating it, the better your prognosis."

Samantha just sat there, not speaking.

"Do you have any questions, Samantha?" Dr. Burke asked her.

"Um, no, not at this time," Sam replied.

"I know this is a lot. I am going to send you home with some brochures and a couple treatment options. Will you come back in a couple days so we can decide on treatment?" Dr. Burke said.

Sam simply nodded, looking dazed.

"I want you to have my direct number, here's the card. Please call me with any questions, alright?" Dr. Burke asked.

"Yes, thank you," Sam said softly.

"Sam, I'm going to have a volunteer sit with you for a bit. I don't want you driving right now, I think you are a little stunned, and I certainly don't blame you. Let me get Catherine to sit with you for awhile," the doctor said.

Catherine, a young girl of about 16 came in to sit with Samantha. Samantha smiled at her and thought how odd it was that this girl is the same age she was when her mom died. And now? Now Samantha has MS. Inconceivable. Suddenly Sam had to get out of that room, out of the doctor's office. Not to go anywhere, she knew she couldn't drive yet, but the walls were closing in on her.

"I know you were supposed to sit with me, but I have to get out of here. I have to go for a walk. I promise that I won't drive, and I'll even leave my purse here if you want, but I have to get out," Sam said to her, nearing hysteria.

"I'd love to walk with you," Catherine said, and followed Sam out to the garden between the buildings. Samantha started walking on the path that wove through the rose bushes. Catherine just followed quietly, never far, and not underfoot.

"Do you garden, Catherine? Do you know how to grow things?" Samantha asked.

"I help my parents garden every year and we grow enough to can for the winter, is that what you mean?" Catherine replied.

"Yeah, I can't grow anything. I plant something, it dies. If someone gives me a plant, it dies, no matter what I do. I wonder if I should have taken that as a sign of things to come...." Samantha trailed off, suddenly very sad.

"Maybe you should take a class on how to take care of plants," Catherine offered.

"It's too late for that," Sam responded.

They walked in silence for a few minutes. Samantha took a deep breath and looked at Catherine, "I think I'm ready to go now, do you think they will let me?"

"Oh sure, they just didn't want you to go when you were upset, let's go get your purse," Catherine responded, turning to go back inside.

Samantha pondered what all this meant as she drove home. There is treatment, she could hold it back for awhile. To what end, she wondered. It was still going to win. She had a terminal illness, and things were out of her control.

Chapter 24

Sam was young when her mother was diagnosed, but she remembered hearing stories later, about how her mom would stagger as she walked and the whole town thought she was a drunk. Sam remembered that within 4 years of being diagnosed, she was bedridden. First she began getting paralyzed on one side, then bedridden, then she could no longer speak, then tube feeding, catheterization, and on and on...

She felt helpless, much like she felt after the doctor told her that Jacob had died but she had to give birth anyway. Life was utterly unfair. Her only consolation was that John was spared from this. She hoped that he had a happy, long life ahead of him. After she got home, she remembered the chart to check off when she ate. She looked in the fridge and nothing at all looked appealing.

Sam decided to order a pizza. She discovered that things seemed different already. Initially, she thought she should get the thin crust vegetarian pizza. However, now, why bother being healthy, Samantha thought. Besides, Dr. Burke wanted her to stop losing weight. Samantha decided to order the spicy hot wings, the all meat pan pizza, and a side salad. She laughed as she realized she probably just ordered enough food for the week. While she waited for the pizza to arrive, she found a blank notebook in her closet and sat down to write.

Sam had no idea what she would write, she just sat down and began filling the pages. The knocking on the door startled her. She jumped up and opened the door for the pizza delivery. Sam was surprised by the young woman who was at her door. She looked like her mom did in the prom photos that she had. Stunned, she just stood there for a moment.

"Did you order pizzas?" the delivery girl said, wondering if she had the wrong house.

"Oh yes, I did, thank you," Sam said, signing the receipt, adding a generous tip.

"Very well, have a good night," she said as she backed away.

Sam shut the door then went to sit the boxes on the countertop. She was still stunned by how much that girl looked like her mom. She shook her head and got a plate out. "I guess we do all have doppelgangers in this world," she said out loud.

As Sam started eating her salad, she thumbed through her notebook. She had already filled a dozen pages, and it seemed to be all about her mom, but written as if her mom were still here. Sam had just picked up the notebook and started writing without thought, so she was shocked to see what she had written. She closed the book abruptly when she found a scene in which her mom was playing with Jacob. Tears flowed down her face.

"Mom is dead, Sam," she reminded herself, "Jacob is dead." Samantha crossed her arms on the table, put her head down on them and sobbed. She realized that she was all alone. She could call John, he would certainly welcome any sign of emotion or neediness in her. That thought just made her cry harder. She missed him so much, yet she had never been what he needed. And now especially, there was no way she would draw him back in.

Without any real thought, Samantha began eating her hot wings and pizza. She was surprised how good everything tasted, and how hungry she was. She felt like she couldn't get enough. Suddenly she remembered that she had a bottle of rum in the cabinet. She poured herself a shot and washed it down with some lemonade that she had in the fridge.

Samantha put a movie in, but it was one that she was extremely familiar with, one that she didn't really have to pay attention to. Background noise, along with something that wasn't so foreign to her, as everything seemed to be lately.

The hot wings were spicy, and she dredged them in a bowl of ranch before eating the meat off of the bone. The pizza tasted amazing to her as well. The pan crust so greasy, the cheese on the edges so crisp, all of the flavors melted together as if someone had discovered the perfect combination of complementary flavors. Samantha felt as if that in itself called for more rum, so she brought the bottle over to the table, along with a large glass of lemonade. She didn't usually eat like this for fear of gaining weight, of being unhealthy. However, since that was no longer an issue, she kept eating, and she kept drinking.

Each bite of the pizza tasted amazing, she could feel each shot of rum pumping through her veins. The movie in the background was a comedy, she found herself laughing along at times. Things didn't seem so bad after all. Good food, good rum, funny movies, what more could a girl want?

"To not be dying, to have a family, to be loved," Samantha answered herself out loud. Suddenly, she felt very ill. She ran to the restroom and barely made it to the toilet before she began throwing up. She held on to the bowl as the wretching continued. She felt tears on her cheeks, the room was spinning, and she could not stop vomiting. Everything that she had eaten came up, then when nothing was left, she continued heaving, fighting to catch her breath between each convulsion.

Afterwards, Sam laid on the floor with her head on the cool tile. She couldn't move, her body ached too much, and when she raised her head, the room began spinning. Samantha fell asleep there, on her bathroom floor, with the movie repeating in the background, too exhausted to be miserable. Sometime in the night, she woke and went to bed, still in the same clothes which looked like she felt, crumpled and old.

She woke with a start, looking around, wondering where she was. After a few moments, she remembered, she was in her new apartment, which currently smelled like pizza and vomit. Samantha pulled the covers over her head to block out her reality. She fell back asleep and awoke hours later, totally rested, with a horrible headache. Sam washed some acetaminophen down with a glass of water and got in the shower. The hot water felt heavenly pouring over her body. She stood there for what seemed like an eternity, then proceeded to wash her hair and scrub her body. Sam combed the conditioner through her hair, ensuring that it wouldn't tangle afterwards.

After the shower, Samantha dressed in an old t-shirt and shorts. Her plan was to scrub the apartment, removing all signs and smells of last night. She scrubbed the toilet, wiped everything down in the bathroom, then mopped the floor. Then she moved to the bedroom where she had to strip the sheets off the bed and toss them in the washing machine. She didn't remember vomiting in her hair, however, the sheets and pillowcase indicated that she had. Samantha lit candles and opened windows as she went.

Finally, she went into the dining room and threw away all signs of dinner. Pizza box, the salad container, the box of hot wing bones, all went into the garbage. Sam loaded the dishwasher, took out the garbage, then wiped down the dining room and kitchen and mopped the floor. When she moved into the living room, she realized it was not affected by last night's activities. The television, however, was still on, with the movie menu on the screen. Samantha took the movie out, put it in it's case and turned the tv off.

Chapter 25

As Sam walked back to the kitchen to get a glass of ice water, she saw her notebook on one of the chairs. She must have tossed it there last night. Sam remembered journaling before the pizza arrived, and she remembered looking through it later and it upsetting her. She tucked it under her arm and carried it to the living room with her. Samantha curled up on the couch and began to read. She remembered it bothering her last night and was trying to be objective today.

She journaled as if her life were perfect, creating an alternate reality in a sense. In her journal, she was married to John, Jacob was a boisterous, excitable boy, and her mom was a doting grandmother. It pained her to read, but she kept on, reading through all of the pages. She didn't remember writing it, and that scared her.

Samantha decided to go for a walk, her apartment seemed so confining all of a sudden. She needed to know there was life outside of these walls, since there seemed to be very little life within them. She blew out all of the candles before she left, grabbing only her keys to take with her. Sam headed out the door, and as a second thought, grabbed her notebook and pen.

Her feet instinctively headed to her new favorite spot, the bench in the cemetery. She sat down and looked at the grave before her. There were fresh flowers on Barbara's grave. That confused Samantha. She wondered who had been here, and why did they put flowers on her grave. Sam looked around, wondering if someone would show up to visit this grave today. She couldn't fathom who that would be.

Sam went over and sat by the grave, tracing the letters that made up her mother's name. She pulled out her pen, opened her notebook and began to write, leaning against the headstone as she did so. Before she knew it, the sky was beginning to darken. Clouds had moved in and she heard thunder. Samantha ran home as the downpour started, twisting her ankle as she darted up the stairs to her apartment. Sam quickly sat down on the steps, catching her breath and checking her ankle. She realized the futility of this situation. There was no one waiting to help her into the apartment, nobody who would go shopping for her, not a soul who would bring her dinner so she could prop her leg up. Most disturbing, though, there was no one who cared.

Samantha sat on the steps, with tears running down her cheeks, falling down onto her notebook for awhile, long enough for the sky to lighten up as the clouds rolled by. Taking a deep breath, she got up and hobbled the rest of the way up the stairs to her apartment. Unlocking the door, she felt totally alone. In a way, she was thankful, and felt like she deserved to be all alone. John had loved her. Jacob had left her. Her mom had left her. The only commonality there was her, and she didn't deserve them in her life.

Sam got a package of frozen peas out of her freezer and sat on the couch with her foot on the coffee table. She put a kitchen towel on her ankle and draped the peas across it. She sat back and closed her eyes. "How did I get here," Samantha wondered. She sighed and opened up her notebook to write some more. Sam had read somewhere about stream of consciousness journaling, and that is what seemed to be coming so naturally lately, except, of course, that what she wrote seemed to be some alternate universe of her life. A best case scenario of sorts.

Samantha's stomach rumbled and she remembered that there was no food in the house, well, not enough to create a meal anyway. If she had put the pizza away properly, she would have had a couple more meals out of it, but it was thrown away this morning. She realized that often she was her own worst enemy. Sam stood and tried to put weight on her foot. Her ankle screamed in pain. Sighing, she hopped to the bathroom to get an ace bandage and sat on the edge of the tub to wrap it. It was swollen and purple, but she could tell it was just a sprain. The longer she could keep it elevated and iced the better. However, now she needed to go to the store.

Samantha planned several meals and made a list of items she would need. She had some time off from work, so she could keep her leg elevated after this shopping trip. She drove to the store, thankful that she could still do that. She made sure that she had all the items in each section before moving on to the next. Sam wanted to walk as little as possible. She got enough for the week's menu and went through the checkout. If she forgot anything, that would be too bad, because she was going to be homebound for awhile. Sam normally didn't let anyone help her with her groceries, but today she happily accepted the help. This shopping trip was exhausting and Sam was ready for a nap.

When she got home, she had to get her groceries up the stairs into her apartment. Samantha started with carrying as much as she possibly could to make fewer trips, however, one of the bags broke on the first trip, spilling canned goods over the lawn. Sam kept going, afraid of stopping altogether, leaving the cans in the grass. She hobbled up the steps, cursing under her breath as she tried to balance on one foot, holding all of her bags. Samantha was near toppling over, trying to get the key in the lock, when her upstairs neighbor walked by and reached over to balance her. The feel of his hands on her waist startled her.

Samantha gasped, and the neighbor stabilized her, keeping her from falling over.

"Thank you, I sprained my ankle and was trying to not put weight on it," Sam said.

"I'm Rick, I should have introduced myself to you sooner. I've seen you coming and going. But anyway, it's nice to meet you," Rick said.

"I'm Sam," she stammered, "it's um, nice to meet you."

"Let me get the groceries you dropped, you should probably get off of your feet," Rick said, and headed out to the grass, not waiting for an answer.

Sam left her door open and hobbled into her kitchen with the bags she had. She started to put her food away, but realized that she was exhausted and sat down at the table. Rick came in with an armful of canned goods.

"You must be tired, can I help you put these away? You should probably elevate your ankle," he said, and started to put the groceries on the counter, again not waiting for an answer.

"I can put stuff away later, thank you," Sam said, moving her foot up into the other kitchen chair. She winced in pain, hoping that Rick didn't notice, but seeing that he did.

"I got all of your refrigerator and freezer stuff put away, the rest is on the counter so you don't have to maneuver around too much, but I'm going to leave you to rest. It was great meeting you, Sam! If you need anything at all, grab your broom and hit it on your ceiling, my floor, ok?" Rick said as he headed to the door. Again, he didn't wait for a response, and was gone before she could say anything.

Samantha hobbled over and locked the door, then laid down on the couch to rest. She made sure her foot was elevated, and remembered nothing more. She woke hours later, hungry and wondering what time it was. She looked at the clock and realized that it was past dinner time. Sam realized that she had not eaten all day. She limped into the kitchen and put a dab of olive oil in a pan. Samantha put three chicken breasts into the pan and seasoned with pepper and garlic. The smells that filled her apartment were heavenly. While they cooked, Sam cut up lettuce, bell pepper, cucumber and put it on a plate. She then sprinkled the salad with blue cheese. When the chicken was done cooking, she set it on the cutting board to rest. Sam poured herself a glass of wine.

Sam diced a chicken breast and put the other two in a covered bowl in the fridge. She added her diced chicken to her salad and poured balsamic vinaigrette over it. She had to carry her wine glass and her plate separately to the table so she didn't spill as she hobbled over. The salad tasted heavenly to Samantha, who had not realized just how hungry she was. She looked around the apartment. The only mess was in the kitchen.

Cleaning wasn't a priority, so she decided she would soak in a warm bath and clean herself up. She could wash her hair tomorrow, but she hadn't bathed since yesterday morning. That means she had not figured out the best way to get in and out of the tub with her ankle. Getting in was easy enough, but after the second glass of wine and the relaxing bath, getting out was proving to be difficult.

After several attempts that needed her to put her weight on one leg, and then the other, in order to get out, she decided to think about how she would instruct the residents at work to manage this. They needed to get out without hurting themselves. It suddenly occurred to her to sit on the side of the tub and move her legs over that way, which didn't require her weight to be on her ankle. After the bath, she wrapped a towel around herself and fumbled her way to the bedroom.

Samantha found herself exhausted again. She laid on the bed, putting an extra pillow under her ankle, which was throbbing. Sam grabbed her journal from her bedside table, along with her pen, and started writing.

The words flowed out of her. She filled page after page, writing about her life, John, her mom, Jacob, even vacations and dream homes. Sam wrote as if it was all her reality. She had an amazing life in her journal. Perfect health, no money woes, and while she wrote it, she was in that reality. Samantha felt like it was harder and harder to pull herself out of that world. She could feel it all the way to her core.

When she journaled about holding Jacob, she could feel it in her soul. Her journal contained all of the secrets of that life, not just all the happy times but it also contained the tales of Jacob's sleepless nights, of John having to work extra hours, of her mom dropping in unannounced. In her journal, Sam painted beautifully and was working on a show in a local, posh gallery. She helped to support the family with her art, and was planning a family trip to Paris to deliver one of her paintings. Samantha fell asleep while she journaled, which only made her fantasy world seem like more of a reality.

Sam dreamed of befriending a woman who was just diagnosed with MS, who was recently divorced, who had lost a child. She was sad for this friend, and decided to take her under her wing, as it were. Sam's new friend was dying, and she needed someone strong like Samantha to help her through. Samantha's heart hurt for this friend, and she had pledged to do all she could to help her.

Chapter 26

The next afternoon, Rick stopped by to check on her. When he knocked on the door, mid-morning, Samantha stumbled over to the door. She had figured that it was someone who was mistakingly knocking, since she didn't really know anyone. When she opened the door, she was surprised to see him.

"Oh, hi," Samantha stammered.

"I just wanted to stop by and see if you needed anything," Rick said as he came into her apartment.

"I'm alright," Sam said.

"I see you are getting around alright, but at least let me make you something to eat. I'm a sous chef, I don't believe that I've mentioned that. What would you like?" Rick rambled off as he looked through her cabinets.

"I see you have all the ingredients here for grilled tuna and green beans. Would you like me to make that?" he continued.

"Sure, as long as you will join me," Sam responded, "I've been getting a little stir crazy lately."

"I would be glad to join you," Rick said, "where is your olive oil? And your garlic?"

Sam pointed him towards her cabinet for the olive oil and towards her counter for a clove of garlic. Rick maneuvered her kitchen like a pro. He easily found the knives, the cutting boards, the bowls. He made a marinade for the tuna with soy sauce, pineapple juice, brown sugar, garlic and pepper. He also diced some garlic and put in a bowl with a tablespoon of olive oil for the green beans. Rick maneuvered around the kitchen as if it were his own, and that thought made Samantha laugh out loud, as she remembered he lived in the same apartment complex and his kitchen was undoubtedly identical to hers.

"What's so funny?" he asked from the kitchen.

"Oh, I was thinking that you looked at home in that kitchen, then chuckled as I realized yours is set up the same way," Sam said.

"Yeah, the people in charge of designing apartments left no room for variations in the floor plan, that's for sure, but it helps me to know where stuff is here. Surprisingly we have just about everything stored in the same places," Rick responded.

He grilled the tuna and somehow sauteed the green beans at the same time. He urged Sam to rest her ankle and wait for dinner. Rick looked through her wine selection and chose one that would complement the dinner.

"Are you on any medication that would keep you from having a glass of wine?" he asked her.

"Um, why would you ask that?" Sam said, startled.

"I just wondered if you were on pain meds for your ankle, sometimes mixing those with alcohol can be a very bad idea and doesn't lend itself well to healing," Rick said.

"Oh. That. No, I'm not on any medications, and I would love some wine with dinner. It smells amazing, by the way," Samantha responded.

"Just a little while longer and we can eat," he assured her.

Sam closed her eyes and relaxed, enjoying the smells coming from her kitchen. She remembered when John would cook for her. He didn't often cook, but when he did, she always felt like the food tasted better than if she had made it. John seemed more adventurous in the kitchen, smelling, adding spices, trying new things, constantly evolving and never creating the same thing twice. She smiled at that memory.

Memories were a funny thing, she thought. Many having the ability to make you smile and cry at the same time. She loved the memory of John cooking for her. A tear rolled down her cheek at the realization that he would never cook for her again.

"Dinner's ready!" Rick called from the kitchen

Sam quickly wiped her tears away and moved to get up off of the couch. Rick rushed over to help her up.

"Don't put any pressure on that ankle, it seems to be healing really well," he said, assisting her off the couch, "lean on me, I've got you."

Sam did exactly as he asked, leaning into him as they walked the few feet to the dining room. She sighed, realizing it has been awhile since she had touched anyone. The feeling was over all too soon as he led her to her chair. The food he had prepared looked amazing and without Sam even noticing he had lit candles on the table. The meal seemed very romantic, and she was amazed at how good everything tasted. When dinner was over, they had downed the entire bottle of wine.

"You are looking really tired, can I help you to bed?" Rick said.

Samantha looked at him, incredulously.

"Um, I didn't mean anything by that. I don't want you stumbling and re-injuring your ankle, and you've had a bit of wine," Rick said.

"Are you trying to seduce me?" Sam said, slurring as she said the word 'seduce'.

"Oh, no, I'm not at all!" Rick responded, "I saw that you weren't getting around and thought I would help you out a bit. My girlfriend went out of town with her mom, so I figured tonight we could have dinner together, enjoy each other's company, and not be lonely. That is all."

"Oh, that's so sweet of you," Sam slurred as they reached the bed. Rick tried to set her down gently but she basically flopped down on the bed and fell over. He thought about helping her get settled but when Rick heard snoring, he just moved her legs up onto the bed and tossed a blanket over her. He then went into the kitchen and cleaned up all the mess for dinner, and locked the door on his way out.

Chapter 27

Samantha spent the final day of her break journaling. Her ankle was almost completely better and she was getting stir crazy, yet she didn't want to risk an injury so she stayed inside. When her stomach growled she looked at her watch and was shocked that she had been writing all day. She decided to order some Chinese food and continue writing. As she waited for her kung pao chicken to arrive, she poured herself some wine and sat back down to write.

In her story, Jacob was going to school. His first day in kindergarten was upon them and he was such a brave boy, he didn't even cry when she dropped him off. She did, of course, but she didn't let him see that. She cried most of the time that he was in school that first day, she missed her little guy so much. Sam counted down the time until she could pick him up. She could've put Jacob on the bus but that simply wouldn't do.

Sam realized that in her story, she was a stay at home mom. John had an amazing job that allowed him to work from home, and together they raised Jacob. Sam's mom had moved nearby and often watched Jacob so they could have a date night. Jacob adored his grandmother. She often joined them to play with Jacob in the park and loved to take him swimming. Samantha was working on a scrapbook for her Mom for Christmas. She was also working on a special gift for her mom from Jacob. He loved his Nana.

Sam jumped with the knock on the door. She loved her peace and quiet so much that there was a stark contrast when something disturbed her. She jumped up to get the food from the delivery driver. She dished out her kung pao and fried rice onto a plate and sat down with her wine. She thought about her story and tears rolled down her face. Her heart ached for

Jacob. She thought for a moment that she would be better off if she stopped writing, if she would let him go, but she just couldn't. He visited her in the story, just as her mom did, and she couldn't live without either one of them. She wouldn't.

She continued writing deep into the night, grateful that she worked a swing shift tomorrow at work. She generally didn't prefer that shift, but it was nice to be able to stay with Jacob and her mom awhile longer. Samantha was starting to feel lost when she didn't have them with her, when she wasn't writing. She struggled with leaving her writing to go to work the next day. Sam decided to take her journal and leave it in the car. If she found any free time, she would write, and she would know it was close.

Chapter 28

"Good morning Sam! How is your ankle?" Jack greeted her as she walked in.

"It's much better, thank you," Samantha replied

"Glad to hear it! Sandra said that she would like to see you when you get in," he said.

"Oh, ok. I hope everything is alright with her. Were there any emergencies while I was off?" Samantha asked, worried.

"No, nobody died, no-one was hospitalized, it's been really quiet around here, actually. I got the impression that she just wanted to check on you, actually. Sandra has told me that she sees a lot of herself in you and she would love to see you become a nurse. Have you thought about that possibility?" Jack said.

"Oh yes, I've thought about it, and at one time I really wanted that. However, I really don't think it's in the cards for me now, Jack. A lot has changed. I don't think I would make a good nurse anymore," Sam said, "is there anything else? I should probably get started."

"No, that was all. Glad to have you back, Samantha," Jack replied.

Sam knew that Sandra would want to talk about her diagnosis. She knew Sam was having tests done, and she knew that Samantha would have the results back by now. If she could avoid Sandra she would, but that would not be possible, so she went directly to the med room. May as well get this over with.

"Hey Sandra, Jack said you wanted to see me?" Sam said as she entered the room and shut the door.

"Yeah, thanks for stopping in. I was wondering how the tests went, and how you are feeling," Sandra said.

"You had already figured it out, right? I have MS. It is most likely relapsing-remitting. I have had only a few episodes of dizziness since I saw you last, however, I am scared of driving, I may start taking public transport soon. I can't even imagine what would happen if I got dizzy while I was driving, you know?" Sam rambled.

"Have you started treatment?" Sandra asked.

"No, I haven't yet. I need to make an appointment. When I was in the doctor's office, receiving my diagnosis, I basically fled. I had to get out of there, I couldn't breathe. They wouldn't let me leave, even assigned me a babysitter. So I walked in the garden and then left," Sam told her.

"You need to start treatment, Sam," Sandra said, "it's your only chance at keeping hold of your quality of life. Right now it's all up to you. You could keep avoiding it and decline rapidly, or you could be proactive and hold it off."

"I know, and I will make an appointment soon. The thing is, either way I'm dying, right?" Sam said.

"We're all dying, Sam. I could be killed during my morning jog tomorrow," Sandra responded, "we just have to make sure that each day is the best it can be, and we don't have any regrets."

"I know. I will make the appointment and get started on treatment. Do you have any insight on what route I should take?" Sam asked

"Do you have an issue with needles?" Sandra asked her.

"No, I don't," Sam responded

"Then I have heard a lot of good things about Avonex. It is an injection. They have had good results," Sandra said.

Samantha thought about that throughout the rest of her shift. She had already done her own research and knew of Avonex. A weekly shot into her thigh or some other fatty area.

116

She could manage that. Samantha walked down the hall to Ethel's room, shaking her head. She wasn't sure why she was choosing to stick herself once a week. It would hold the MS back, maybe. It would prolong her life, maybe. But there were no guarantees.

"Hey Ethel, how are you? Are you ready for your shower?" Sam asked as she arrived in the room. As soon as she saw Ethel though, she knew that things weren't ok with her. She was sitting in her recliner, with her head tossed back, mouth gaping open, and sweating profusely. "Ethel! I need you to wake up Ethel!" she yelled as she felt for a pulse. Ethel was breathing and there was a pulse. However, Sam still couldn't get Ethel to respond. She pulled the pull cord in Ethel's room and in her bathroom. That was the signal that there was an emergency. The rest of the staff would be alerted on their pagers, and one would bring Sandra.

Sam grabbed Ethel's bedside glucometer and pricked her finger to test. Sam gasped as the number came on the screen, just as Sandra entered the room.

"26, Sandra, we need to give her some glucose and call 911," Sam said, her voice shaking.

"Her Glucagon pen is in her nightstand, let me get it," Sandra said as she injected it into Ethel's thigh, "come on Ethel, you are just having some low blood sugar, we are giving you your Glucagon to raise it, it's time to wake up."

Sandra got her blood pressure cuff and stethoscope and checked Ethel's blood pressure, "please count her respirations," she said to Sam as she checked. "Her color is returning a bit. Her BP is not terrible, and I think she is going to be ok," Sandra said as the paramedics came in.

Sam briefed them on finding Ethel and told them what they had done. Ethel was starting to stir a bit as they loaded her onto the gurney.

"Ethel, your blood sugar dropped. We gave you some glucose, but they are going to check you out at the hospital. We will call your son and take care of Boo while you are gone, but you will be back soon, ok?" Sam said to her. In response, Ethel squeezed her hand.

"May as well get all of her linens washed while she is gone," Sam laughed as she stripped the sheets off the bed, "I will also let the housekeeper know that now is her chance to get in here and clean, I know she will appreciate being able to do that without Ethel harping at her!"

"I'm going to go and start charting. Make sure you do your part on that as soon as you can. I will also order another Glucagon pen from the pharmacy" Sandra said, leaving the room.

Sam took the sheets to the laundry room and then went in search of the housekeeper to suggest she get into do a deep clean on Ethel's room while she can. She also asked one of her coworkers to take Boo out. Suzy loved Boo more than any other staff member and welcomed time with her, so she was grateful to be able to do it.

When she arrived at the staff room to do her charting, Sandra was already done. Sam breathed a sigh of relief, shut the door and took out Ethel's chart. Sandra had praised her on her charting before, as she was very concise and put all the facts, leaving out opinion. Sam knew that was a direct result of her training in journalism throughout high school. She looked at her watch. Her shift was almost over. She went into the med room and did all of the follow up charting on the PRN's she had given out, and grabbed her purse.

"Have a good day, Sandra," Sam said, headed to the door.

"You too, and let me know about what we talked about earlier, ok?" Sandra requested.

"Sure thing," Sam said, smiling. Her smile faded as soon as she got out of the building. She knew she would have to make that doctor's appointment. Sandra was going to keep asking and she didn't want to have to avoid her.

Sam dialed Dr. Burke's office on her cell as she walked to the car.

"This is Samantha Green and I need to schedule an appointment with Dr. Burke, please," she said to the receptionist.

"Oh yes, Miss Green, I have your chart right here. What would be a good day for you?" the receptionist replied.

"My next day off is Thursday, does she have any openings early in the day?" Sam asked.

The receptionist asked her to be there at 10:30 Thursday morning and Sam jotted it down as she reached her car. She couldn't trust her memory lately, she had found. Samantha planned her Thursday. She would get up at her normal time, by 7am at the latest, go grocery shopping for the week, put groceries away at home, then go to the doctor. That would free up the rest of the day to do whatever she would like. Of course, she would have to clean a bit, but she could do that whenever. She had Thursday and Friday off. Samantha wondered what side effects her treatment would have. Would she be sore at the injection site? Would it make her nauseated? Would she be tired? Sam wondered if it would affect her mood, and mostly she wondered if it would actually slow the progression down.

Chapter 29

When Sam got home she heated up some soup and sat at the table with her notebook. Her pen seemed to have a life of it's own as she wrote about Jacob and her mom at the pool. Jacob had zinc oxide on his nose, blindingly white in the sun. Samantha had told her mom over and over that they make it in clear now, but her mom was always wanting to use up some old products that she had. Sure it would keep him from getting sunburned but he was the only child there with a white nose. Jacob never seemed to mind, though, and he always acted like his grandmother was the sun, moon and the stars all rolled into one. In fact, at bedtime he always insisted on calling her before getting tucked in. He would argue about going to bed until he could speak to her, then he would go straight to bed with no further arguments.

Samantha realized that in this story, nobody ever got sick. There was no MS, no falling over box fans, no stitches, no death. That made her smile. She had created nirvana. Sam realized, as a tear rolled down her face, that she would dive in if she could.

John loved to give Jacob baths and had bought him toys: sharks, submarines, even dinosaurs for his bath. They would often be in there for an hour or more, creating entire scenarios around his toys. John would begin by telling a story that he had worked on that day and Jacob's imagination would take over. Sam often sat outside the bathroom listening to them as they played. The dinosaurs would often attack the sharks, but then the submarines would fire on the dinosaurs and save the sharks. Sam would have to mop up the bathroom each night, and she loved nothing more.

At night, as the house slept, sexual hunger would awaken within Samantha and John. They would often make love for hours, by candlelight in their bedroom. They had a bond that could not be broken and even though they had been having sex with one another for years, it never got old, and was always the most exciting sex of their lives, every single time.

John got the bulk of his work done in his office, while Jacob was at school. If he was still working when she went to pick Jacob up she would take him to the park or to the mall with her mom. Jacob always had a lot of energy and enjoyed playing with the other children. Jacob was a very kind child and the other kids always seemed to flock to him. He always hugged all of his friends goodbye too, and that warmed Samantha's heart. In fact, Jacob rarely had a tantrum. He had slept through the night at just 8 weeks old, and Sam and John always knew how blessed they were. In fact, now that Jacob was in school, they have been talking about having another baby.

"I don't know, John, what if we have a difficult baby?" Sam said to him one day after John brought up a second child.

"So what? We have more than enough love for another child and Jacob would love to have a baby brother or sister," John said.

"You do have a point. We should start trying, then, shouldn't we? After all, trying is the fun part," Sam responded as she winked at him.

Chapter 30

Thursday morning, Sam was up at 6:45 a.m. which was sleeping in for her. She often wished she could sleep later in the mornings, but she has found recently that she can always take a nap in the afternoon. After her morning routine that involved a shower, and drinking a cup of coffee while doing her hair and makeup.

By 7:30, she was on her way to the store with the week's menu and grocery list. Sam knew that this early on a Thursday, the store would be practically empty, and that is how she preferred it. Samantha detested shopping, and when it was crowded she got anxious and often forgot things on her list, just to get out of there.

Today the store was exactly as she expected. A few people scattered throughout shopping, several employees stocking shelves. Sam breathed a sigh of relief as she made her way throughout the store. She was buying items that she had never bought before, since she was trying to keep weight on, and even gain some. It shouldn't be too hard. Bread, pasta, real cheese, eggs, real butter. Sam chuckled at the fact that she had been denying herself those very things for so long. She was conscientious of the fact that she still needed to eat healthy and bought plenty of vegetables to incorporate into her meals, she just also allowed herself to get her favorite ice cream and ingredients for her favorite cupcake: red velvet with cream cheese frosting. When Samantha reached the cashier and began putting her groceries on the conveyer belt, her arms felt heavy. She reached into her cart for the box of cupcake mix, lifted it to put on the conveyor, and dropped it back into the cart. Sighing, Sam reached for it again and once again dropped it.

Samantha was aware that there was someone in line behind her, and she was also aware that she was taking too long. She had to pick up almost everything twice because she couldn't seem to hold on to it. When she finally got everything on the conveyor, she took a deep breath, afraid to look up into anyone's eyes. Her goal was to get out of there.

"Your total is $72.14, ma'am," the cashier said.

Sam went to swipe her debit card in the terminal, but couldn't seem to get it to slide right. Her hand was shaking and she couldn't control it. She looked at the cashier, pleadingly.

"Can I swipe it for you, ma'am?" the cashier asked, her hand extended. She had kind eyes and Sam was so grateful to her. Sam handed her card over to her. "Here's your receipt, Brandon will help you take your groceries out, have a good day."

Samantha simply nodded, thankful for not having to ask for help.

After he placed the groceries in her trunk, Brandon asked "are you alright to drive?"

"Yes, I was just a little shaky. I will be fine, thank you," Samantha answered.

After he walked off, Sam started crying. She knew that she needed to calm herself before driving and wondered if she was indeed alright to drive. Samantha realized that she was here, with ice cream in her trunk, and she had no choice. She took a deep breath and started the car. She took back roads back home and avoided all traffic. When she got there, she unloaded her groceries without incident and put them away as well. Her hands weren't shaky, she had no issues with gripping the items. Sam completed the tasks with gratitude and then drove to her doctor's appointment.

"How've you been doing, Samantha?" Dr. Burke asked her.

"I've been fine," Samantha responded.

"Ok, let's cut to the chase, what has been going on with you? Last time I saw you, I diagnosed you with MS and you were understandably upset. We had also discovered that you had been losing weight, and I asked you to track your meals. How have you been feeling? How is your memory? Your energy level? I see that you've actually gained a little of the weight back and that is awesome!" Dr. Burke said.

"Since I was here, I tripped and sprained my ankle, took some time off work, ate a lot, and haven't really noticed many symptoms. Until this morning," Sam replied.

"Tell me about what happened this morning," Dr. Burke coaxed.

"I was in the grocery store. I get overwhelmed in crowds, so I went early. I got up to the register and started putting my groceries on the conveyor and I kept dropping things. I couldn't get a grip on anything. And when it came time to swipe my debit card, I couldn't control the shaking of my hand enough to do it. The cashier had to do it for me. Thankfully I was calm enough to drive home, but I did take back roads to avoid traffic. By the time I got home, I was fine," Sam told her as Dr. Burke wrote notes in her book.

"Do you have a support system in place, Samantha?" the doctor asked.

"No, not really. I don't have family, and I don't know a lot of people," Sam responded.

"As you know, with relapsing-remitting MS, your symptoms will come in waves, then fade away again, much like they did this morning. With no treatment, the waves will come more quickly and they will fade more slowly. The symptoms will be debilitating a lot sooner. I would like to talk to you about a treatment called Avonex. This is an injectible medication, so you would need to be able to give yourself a shot once a week, do you think that you could do that?" Dr. Burke asked her.

"I was talking with our RN at work about Avonex and I could give myself a shot, yes. She had me practice with some saline, actually," Samantha responded.

"Wow, that is good, so it does sound like you have a little bit of a support system in place, if you can talk with your RN," the doctor said.

"Oh, yes, I hadn't thought about that. Sandra is very helpful, yes," Sam said.

"I will give you a prescription for Avonex, then, and your kit will be delivered by one of their representatives. They want to make sure you have the best start with the med. During the first four shots, the first month of your treatment, they will be titrating your dose up. They have found that there are fewer side effects that way, and after that they have a pen to deliver the med, you won't even have to see the needle. One of their reps will be calling you to schedule a visit and you can have them meet you at work or at home. You will want a place for some privacy though since you will be giving yourself a shot in your thigh or another fatty area. Now, I would like to talk to you about a support group. We have a very active chapter of the National MS Society here and I urge you to get in touch with them, try out a meeting, talk with them. It is helpful to have others around you who are going through the same thing as you are," Dr. Burke said.

"I will look into that. It seems like everything is happening so fast," Samantha said.

"I know it's all overwhelming, and things will calm down, but you've already made a lot of good choices, the choice to come in and be tested, and the choice to start treatment, along with the choice to eat better to get some weight on. If you continue to make good choices, then you will do fine. Please do talk with the MS Society though. They will be an invaluable resource," Dr. Burke replied.

Sam left with a prescription for Avonex, a brochure about relapsing-remitting MS, and a brochure detailing what the National MS Society does. It wasn't even noon and Sam was exhausted. Her morning had been frustrating, terrifying, and tiring. She wept as she remembered her experience in the checkout line at the grocery store. Samantha had not felt that helpless in a very long time. She was also fearful about when other symptoms came. Was each one going to be so unnerving? What if she got dizzy while driving? What if she embarrassed herself in public again, having everyone stare at her like she was sure they had done in the checkout line?

Sam decided to take a nap when she got home. She realized she hasn't eaten anything today, but decided that rest was more important. She would make up for it with lots of food later, and hopefully she would be able to go for a walk.

Her short nap turned out to be two hours long. She was shocked when she looked at the clock, but there was still time to do the things she had planned. First, she needed to eat, she woke up starving. Sam got out a hamburger patty and some bacon. She had been craving a good, juicy cheeseburger for what seemed like forever. Samantha had always denied herself such things so she could keep from gaining weight. Now that wasn't an issue, she wanted nothing more than this burger. Sam didn't have a barbecue grill so she cooked the bacon then drained the excess grease and then cooked the patty. She found herself wishing that she had mushrooms, and made a mental note to get some next time.

Sam poured herself some iced tea and sat down to eat her burger. She began to think about what had happened in the grocery store this morning. Samantha wondered if Avonex would indeed slow down the progression of her MS. Even if it did, what did that mean for her? That she may have four good years left instead of two? That she may have twenty good years left? She knew there was no way of knowing. She also knew that if it came down to her totally relying on others for care, she wanted to end it on her terms. Samantha had researched physician assisted suicide, and felt strongly about having that choice. She was proud to live in Oregon where such a thing was not only legal but possible. Sam knew there was a process to work through in order to have the right to die and made a mental note to prepare for that.

The cheeseburger tasted delicious to Sam. She had put just the right combination of mayonnaise, mustard, lettuce, pickle, and bacon. Samantha devoured the burger as if she had been starving. In a way, she realized that she had indeed been starving herself for years. She had made an art form out of denying herself many of her favorite foods, relationships with any depth (both romantic and platonic), she even denied herself nice clothes and home decor because she didn't feel worthy. While she enjoyed every single bite of her burger, she thought of the ways that she had robbed herself of love. Her entire life. She had taken a life that had the potential to be rich and deep, and she made something that was two dimensional and grey.

Sam knew that there was no one to blame but herself. She would like nothing more than to blame her mom for dying, or John for not pushing her harder to come out of her shell. At the end of the day, though, she was a stubborn girl and she made her choices. She alone built the walls, day by day, until she was imprisoned in her own fortress.

Samantha walked to the cemetery after she cleaned up her mess from lunch. She felt good, not at all wobbly, but she instinctually grabbed her cellphone on her way out the door in case anything happened. As she walked, she wondered who she would call if she became unstable, or if she fell, or if she somehow couldn't make it back. Sam couldn't think of a single person that would help her. She could call Sandra, she supposed, but theirs was more of a professional relationship and this would be far too private. She wasn't close to anyone else at work and certainly couldn't call John. Sam thought that maybe she should join the support groups for others with MS so that she had someone that she could call on in emergencies, and maybe so that she could have a friend who understood.

Chapter 31

At the cemetery, Sam automatically went to the bench by Barbara's grave. She sat there for a few minutes, mentally deciding when she would contact the MS Society. Samantha struggled with the decision to reach out to anyone, as she has always plowed through on her own. Suddenly, however, she felt quite small and was unsure of her own ability to get through this. Sam got up to walk through the headstones. She ran her fingertips along them as she walked by. She had always felt at home in the cemetery. Suddenly she became sad, she felt like her life had been built like a house of cards and it was crashing down now. Samantha was surprised by a tear rolling down her cheek. She wandered back to Barbara's headstone and sat down, sobbing by the time she arrived there. She found herself talking to the headstone.

"I don't have anyone. I haven't built relationships, I am not important to anyone. I have become a pro at building walls and pushing people away. And now, I'm dying. What the hell has been the point? There will be no one left to mourn me when I'm gone. Nobody will remember me after I die, no one will tell my stories or recall what I meant to them. My headstone will just be overcome with weeds and will fade away, forgotten. What is the damn point?" Samantha was shouting and slamming her fists on the headstone as she finished.

"Is everything alright, Ma'am?" Sam heard, startling her. She looked up and saw the groundskeeper, looking at her.

"Oh, yes, sorry. Everything is fine," she said as she stood up, "everything is going to be alright" she said, walking away, "everything is going to be just fine."

Samantha walked home, wiping her nose and sniffling. She knew what she had to do. Sam felt more determined than ever. She noticed the sunset as she walked. It was gold and orange and made her hopeful. The sun moved gracefully into the horizon and she realized that she could too, and she will, with or without leaving anyone to mourn her. Samantha had wasted her entire life, and it was time to start living it. When she got home, Sam went straight to her journal. She picked it up and moved to thumb through it, she stopped herself and threw it in the garbage. Sam realized that she needed to let the past go in order to move forward.

Sam ate a steak and baked potato for dinner. She had worked up an appetite with her walk, and crying always made her both exhausted and hungry. After dinner, she poured a glass of wine and got out her painting supplies. Samantha had a few unpainted canvases that were begging to be made into works of art. She felt like she effectively replicated tonight's sunset, looking at her paintings made her feel alive.

Suddenly, she was anxious to start her treatment. Sam was ready to live, and ready to push death away. She certainly wasn't ready for it to be over. Her next painting was vibrant colors, and signified her newly electrified soul. Before bed she had a third artwork started, and she only went to bed because it needed to dry a bit and she needed to buy more canvas.

Chapter 32

Work was going well for Sam the next day, Ethel was back from the hospital and was thankful to the staff for taking care of Boo for her. As she was preparing the meds, Sandra was hovering in the med room the whole time. When she was walking around the dining room giving meds, Sandra was in the doorway of the med room watching her. Samantha had no idea what was going on, but when breakfast was over, Sandra was nowhere to be found. Sam headed to Jack's office to get to the bottom of this.

"Jack, do you have any idea what Sandra's deal is?" Sam asked as she pushed the door open, and as she stepped in, she saw Sandra sitting there.

"Oh, I was looking for you," Sam said.

"I came in here to have a meeting with Jack, and it's just as well that you are here," Sandra said, "why don't you have a seat?"

"Alright, what's going on?" Sam said as she looked at Jack pleadingly. He simply motioned his hand towards an empty seat.

Samantha's stomach churned as she sat down. She couldn't get fired. "Oh please don't let me get fired," she thought to herself.

"I've just been talking to Jack about your diagnosis," Sandra said to her.

"Is that not confidential, Sandra? I had confided in you, and I really don't understand why you two are in here discussing my health," Sam replied.

"Ok, we are off to a bad start here. Can we just begin again?" Jack said.

"Samantha, I wasn't trying to break a confidence, in fact, I thought long and hard before I even came to Jack. However, as you know, Multiple sclerosis can affect not only your physical abilities, but also your cognition. And the fact is, you are operating under my license," Sandra said.

"I understand, Sandra, but I don't understand why you didn't talk to me, why you didn't ask me if I could still do the job," Sam said, almost pleading with her.

"I haven't told you, but my sister has relapsing remitting MS," Sandra said, "and I've watched how it can progress. It doesn't always go the same way, but the fact is that it can."

"I'm starting on Avonex this week. I have four doses to titrate it up, then I'll be on a maintenance dose. I'm sure that I will have bad days and good days, but don't we all?" Samantha asked her.

"We will do everything to support you, and likely you will be able to work for a long time, however, I'm going to take you off of meds. I just can't have you working under my license when you are struggling with this," Sandra said to her.

"Sam, your job is not in jeopardy. You simply won't be dispensing meds any longer. You know that Sandra is making the best choice for her license," Jack added

"Thank you for that. I'm glad I still have a job. And I will prove to you that you made a good choice to keep me. I will miss doing meds, but I understand," Sam replied.

"Sam, if you need anything at all, please let me know. If you aren't feeling well, come talk to me, alright?" Jack said.

"Ok, but I feel fine, just want you to know that," Samantha said.

"You haven't been looking so great lately, in all honesty, Sam," Sandra said, "we have both been worried about you for awhile now."

"I appreciate your concern, but I think things are going to be better now," Sam said, and as she heard herself say those words, she knew they were true, but she could see that they weren't convinced, "I know that you both have doubts, and that's ok. You'll see, everything will be alright."

"Just remember, we are here if you need us," Jack said, "now get back to work!"

Chapter 33

After work, Sam decided to stop by the craft store. She wandered through the aisles for an hour before settling on a couple new brushes and five canvases of varied sizes. Samantha also decided to buy some acrylic paints for some ideas she had. She also decided to go through the drive through on the way home as well, since she was hungry and didn't want to spend time cooking. In fact, all she wanted to do was change into her favorite old shirt and dive in to her paintings.

She had an idea for a painting, that if executed well might look like tie-dye. At least, in her mind it did. She was anxious to see if it would actually work. Sam prepped the canvas with the palest of blues. You could barely see a tint to it. Once it was dry, she laid the canvas flat on her table and watered down red, blue and yellow paint each in their own bowls. She then got out some medicine droppers that the lady at the craft store recommended and a straw. She put drops of the watered down paint on the canvas and blew it around with a straw. It didn't turn out exactly as she had pictured it, but it was beautiful.

For the first time, she felt like an artist. She stood back and looked at her new painting. She looked at the sunset painting on the easel. Sam hadn't realized it, but she had her paintings hanging all over her apartment. She also had not realized just how talented she was. Her paintings were gorgeous! Sam momentarily felt bad for her lack of humility about this, however, she quickly began dreaming about getting her art out there into the world. She poured a glass of wine and walked through her apartment, looking at all the paintings, pretending like she was at a posh gallery show. She looked at her work critically, and realized that she needed to paint the edges of her canvases to finish them, and she needed to come up with a signature and sign her work.

So far Samantha had seventeen finished paintings, and had four blank canvases to work on. That would be twenty one completed works, once they were all completed to satisfaction. She remembered that one of the resident's daughter managed a gallery downtown. Sam wondered if she were brave enough to contact her about having a show. She decided that she would complete twenty five pieces before she would contact her, and she would complete over thirty prior to the show. Sam had no idea if her numbers were high or low, but it felt right to her. She hoped to finish the four canvases this week and would buy more supplies on payday. She figured that she could easily be done with more than thirty paintings within the month.

The next morning at work, Sam went into Jack's office on her break.

"Hey Jack, can I talk to you?" Sam asked as she entered.

"Sure, Sam, what's going on?" Jack asked, bracing himself for the conversation to come.

"Well, I don't talk much about what I do in my spare time, but I've been painting quite a bit, and I think I'm pretty good," Sam began.

Jack simply looked at her quizzically, still wondering where this was going.

"Well, you know that Connie's daughter runs that gallery downtown right? I'd like to ask her if I can show my work there, but I want to make sure that's alright for me to do first," Sam continued.

"Oh, I see, and that's great, Sam! I don't see how there would be any conflict in that. Please keep me in the loop though, would you? If you show your paintings there, I'd love to go see it and I know my wife would as well. In fact, we might be able to take some of the residents for an outing to see your work as well, or we could even move your work here after the show, if that would interest you. Would likely be great publicity for us as well, to be honest," Jack said.

"Really Jack? Do you mean that? I can show my work here sometime? You have no idea what that would mean to me! And I agree, that an evening welcoming the public in would be great for the facility, and the residents too! They could dress up and help host the event!" Sam said, growing increasingly excited, "but first, I have some more painting to do. Thank you Jack!"

Chapter 34

That evening, Samantha got her acrylics out again. She painted a large canvas black, taking special care on the edges. She made sure there was no canvas showing through at all. While she waited for it to dry, she got a painting off the wall and painted the edges, leaving it on the spare easel to dry. She knew that she would have to get creative about where to place them all to dry, since most of her paintings have not been finished. She also made a mental note to always paint the edges as part of the original process.

Tonight, Sam opened a can of soup for dinner. She had some rolls left from a dinner earlier in the week, and poured a tall glass of iced tea. Samantha made a mental note to get everything for grilled cheese sandwiches and tomato soup for next week. Chicken noodle was good for tonight, though. Sam smiled as she thought of hanging her work in the assisted living facility. She also realized that she felt more alive than she ever had before.

After she ate, Sam cleared off the table. She returned to the black canvas and laid it on her table. She got her white, yellow, red, and electric blue acrylic paints out and watered each one down in it's own bowl. Suddenly, she had an idea, and planned an area that extended over the entire bottom third of the canvas. In the top two thirds, she used the dropper to drop the watered-down paint onto the canvas, and blew through the straw straight down onto the drops. It looked exactly as she had imagined, like fireworks in the night sky. She would have to plan out the bottom and then she knew exactly how she would finish it. The planning would have to happen tomorrow, she realized, as it was getting late. Before bed, she covered the table with waxed paper and laid four canvases down on it. Samantha painted the edges of these four paintings before bed.

Sam went to bed completely satisfied with this day. Samantha decided that tomorrow she would contact Connie's daughter. She was nervous, but decided that if it didn't go well with her, she would approach other galleries, and keep doing it until one said yes. Sam chuckled to herself as she thought that. She had never been persistent, and she certainly had never believed in herself the way she did now.

As she drank her coffee, she looked at her artwork with fresh eyes. Her work was good, really good. She could proudly hang it in any gallery. Sam made a list of how many still needed signatures and how many needed the edges painted. She felt confident in approaching Connie today. Sam decided that she would contact her right after her shift ended. On her way out the door, she snapped a few pictures of her paintings with her cell phone.

"Just in case Connie wants to see some right away," Sam said to herself on the way to work. She thought about her day. She was giving showers today, a task that was infinitely easier now than when she first started. She smiled as she remembered how things were when she first began. In fact, Sam realized how much she had grown in the past couple of years. She had begun this job as a mourning young woman, shortly after Jacob's death. This job has seen her through that dark sadness, the divorce, her diagnosis, and now into what she feels will be an art career. Samantha was walking through the halls reflecting on how far she had come, smiling as she walked. As she turned the corner, she ran right into Gina, Connie's daughter.

They both laughed as they grabbed onto one another for support.

"I hadn't planned to run into you today, Gina, but I'm so glad I did!" Sam said to her.

"Oh yeah, why is that, Sam?" Gina replied

"Well, I am an artist, a painter. I have a whole bunch of paintings and I was hoping to talk to you about possibly showing them in your gallery, if that might be a possibility, you know, at some point," Samantha rambled.

"Are you serious, Sam? I would love to see your work! My gallery loves to represent local artists, and our specialty is discovering new talent! Could it be our secret that it was you who discovered us?" Gina asked, winking, "when can I see your work?"

"I will gladly bring it by the gallery at your convenience, but I do have a few cell phone shots if you'd like to see them," Sam said, "how about I let Jack know I need to take a short break and then we can sit down for a moment?"

"That sounds perfect. Let me tell my mom I'm going to be a few minutes and I will meet you in the dining room, it should be pretty empty right now," Gina said before she turned to go to her mom's room.

Sam practically ran to Jack's office. She was out of breath when she got there and Jack looked concerned as she arrived.

"Oh! Everything's fine! But I wanted to ask if I could go on a break. I ran into Gina upstairs and she wants to see my work. She wants to see my work, Jack! Is it okay that I take a few minutes with her?" Samantha said breathlessly.

Jack laughed, "of course, don't take longer than your break, but yes, you can meet with her."

Without even thinking, Sam hugged him.

"Thank you, Jack! Thank you so much!" Sam said as she ran out of the room.

Jack smiled as she ran out.

As she approached the dining room, she saw Gina looking at some photos on the wall. They were photos of the resident's activities, and her mother was in several of them.

"I think your mom really likes it here," Sam said to her.

"You know, she really does! Can I tell you a secret? I'm really glad she does! She was driving me crazy when we were moving her out of her home," Gina said with a chuckle.

"I can only imagine. Would you like some coffee?" Sam asked as she headed to the coffee pot.

"Oh, I'd love some, thank you! Also, I have my iPad here, I was wondering if you could email me a photo or two of your work so we can look at it on a slightly larger screen than your phone," Gina responded.

"Great idea, let me send them now, then get the coffee just in case it takes a moment to receive them. Cream and sugar?" Sam said.

Sam brought Gina her coffee, along with a pitcher of creamer and an assortment of sweeteners. She sat down and stirred both into her own coffee, feeling her heart pounding in her chest. When Gina picked up her iPad to look at it, Sam thought she would die right then and there. Gina said nothing for a few moments. Sam simply kept stirring her coffee since she seemed unable to do anything more.

"Wow, Samantha. These paintings are beautiful. Would you mind if I stopped by to see them? I will be visiting Mom for the day, so afterwards, if it suits you, I'd love to see them. What is your largest piece?" Gina asked.

"I have several different sizes, but I believe the largest I have right now is 24"x36". I believe 5"x7" is the smallest I have, and the rest are in between," Sam answered.

"I can't commit until I've both seen them and have talked to my team, but I'd love to show your work. However, I want a couple larger pieces, alright? I'm thinking 4'x5' or bigger. Do you think you can manage that? Also, how many completed paintings do you have right now?" Gina asked.

"I have close to 30 right now and I can do as large as you'd like!" Sam replied, thankful to hear confidence in her response since she felt terrified of painting a canvas so large. She was committed now, or at least she should be, she thought. "I'm off at three today and will be home anytime after that, I will email you my address, alright?"

"That sounds perfect, Sam. Thank you for this opportunity to showcase your talent," Gina said, extending her hand.

Stunned, Sam shook her hand "the pleasure is all mine, I assure you, thank you so much and I will see you later!"

Chapter 35

When she got home, she was so thankful that she always kept it tidy. She laid her paintings out, put two up on the easels, and got to work signing what she could while she waited. She looked at her paintings again, trying to be more critical of them. She saw good paintings, she saw talent, and she was very impressed with herself. She was beaming when Gina knocked at the door. Sam ran to the door, took a deep breath and opened it.

"Please, come in," Sam said, feeling like her voice betrayed her nervousness.

Gina nodded, walked in and walked directly over to the paintings. She looked at each one for a few moments, then went on to the next. She paused at the dark acrylic painting and looked confused.

"Is this one unfinished?" Gina asked.

"Yes, my vision is to paint words on it that say Live. Love. Dream. or something similar. With the effect of fireworks above," Sam replied.

"Your choice of writing style will matter. Pick carefully. Can we sit for a few minutes?" Gina said.

"Of course, would you like some juice, or some wine?" Samantha asked her, finally remembering her manners.

"No, thank you, but I am going to take some notes as we talk, I hope you don't mind," Gina said.

They sat on the couch. Sam felt like she was in a job interview, and she basically was. She knew that she had to sell herself now so that Gina could fight for her when she presented the idea to her team. Sam simply nodded.

"Why do you paint, Sam?" Gina began.

"I began painting after my son died. I was almost eight months pregnant and he died. I was lost. We had no indication that anything bad was going to happen. My son's name is Jacob. I had lost sight of beauty in the world, and a coworker took me to a painting class and I dove in. After the first class, I went straight to the art supply store and stocked up. Painting was the only thing that made me feel alive. However, as my marriage was ending, I forgot that for a time. I put away my brushes, I withdrew. Then recently, I was diagnosed with Multiple sclerosis. My mom had MS and I watched her deteriorate before my eyes and initially I braced for impending death. However, let's just say I had an awakening and I have a strong desire now to live my life to the fullest. So, again, painting is saving me, and that's why I paint. Sorry for such a rambling answer," Sam said.

"Wow, Sam, that is quite a story. Do you mind if I share that with my team? Also, would you mind if we shared some of it in promotional materials?" Gina asked.

"That is such a scary question, but no, after all is said and done, I don't mind. I want to live my life out loud, it's about time I did that. It's good to be alive," Sam said.

"That firework painting, Sam. I would like you to finish that one for yourself, to keep. But I also want you to do one super big, 5'x 4' or bigger with the words 'It's Good to Be Alive' at the bottom of that one. Can you do that? I would want that to be the main painting, with all of your others surrounding. And I'm thinking at least forty paintings. What I'm hoping for is a two week long show, with a wine and cheese artist reception where people can meet you," Gina said.

Tears came to Sam's eyes, "You have no idea what this means to me!"

"Your story is quite inspirational, Sam. I am honored to have this chance to see your work. I am sure my team will be in total agreement with me. Do you mind if I snap a few more pictures of your work to show them? I brought my camera with me," Gina asked.

"Of course I don't mind, thank you so much!" Sam replied as Gina got up and began taking pictures of several of her paintings.

"I will let you know what my team says, but in the meantime, I'd get to painting if I were you!" Gina said as she walked towards the door, "thank you for reaching out to me, Sam, I appreciate it."

"Thank you so much Gina, I look forward to hearing from you!" Sam said, then closed the door behind Gina. She turned around, leaned against the door, and took a deep, ragged breath, as she exhaled, she said "wow" and noticed tears on her cheeks. She had been hiding her whole life, she had purposefully been not special, not noticeable. Sam had purposefully not connected with people her whole life. She felt so vulnerable right now, but also alive. Alive in ways that she has never felt before. Sam jumped up and threw her hands in the air, laughing as she did so, thankful that she could, and that her life was turning into something worth living.

Chapter 36

Sam's stomach growled and she realized that she was famished. She considered putting off eating to go to the craft store and buy that large canvas, but she knew she needed to take care of her body so that it would continue to take care of her. Sam compromised and decided to eat at the cafe near the craft store. As she walked in, Sam remembered that this cafe has always felt like home. She remembered the first time she came here with John. Samantha fell in love with the energy here, the quirky cafe with the vertical gardens, the art gallery, and the gift shop. And just like that, Sam knew that she needed to show her work here.

She decided that while she was at the craft store she would buy a new journal. This journal, much unlike the last one, will be about the future, not the past. This journal will be her dreams and goals journal. Sam ate her chicken caesar salad outside in the vertical garden, enjoying the gorgeous sunset. She could see part of the art gallery from where she sat and she dreamed about the day when her work was in there. This was a cafe where you ordered and paid before finding a seat, so when she was done, she cleared her own table and headed out, waving goodbye on her way out the door.

The first item in her cart was a gorgeous blue leather journal with silver leaf on the edge of the pages. The leather was stamped with a leaf pattern and felt so soft and supple in her hands. This is the kind of journal that she would normally be intimidated to write in, wanting the perfect thing to fill it, but she had that covered. She found a 5' x 6' canvas, but discovered two things with the purchase of that tonight. One, she had no idea how to get it home, and two, a canvas this size was a lot more expensive than she had anticipated. Sam knew she had the money for it, but she liked to think about such large purchases before making them, and she needed to figure out how to transport it. Maybe she could bring a blanket to cushion it and tie it on top of her car, she would see if that would be the way to do it. Sam picked up some acrylic paint, she would need large amounts for the large canvas, she decided on royal blue for the background.

She also bought another container of gesso, this time picking the gallon container. Sam smiled as she put that in her cart and realized that she was an artist. She also put mineral spirits and some new brushes in her cart, along with some very small canvases, just for fun. One was 2"x2", a 3"x2", and a 3"x3", all with their own personal easels. Her final addition to her cart was some new drop cloths to protect her apartment from any splatters or spills. Sam paid for her items and headed out to her car. She was thankful to be able to buy art supplies, to be able to thrive despite all of the choices she had made prior.

As she approached her car, she became dizzy and stumbled, banging her shoulder into the car door. Her knee hit the pavement, and she scraped her the knuckles of her right hand on the parking lot as she tried to not lose her bag or break anything in it. She eased herself to the ground and checked herself for injuries. Her hand was bleeding a little bit, but it was just scraped. Her wrist may be sprained, but she was certain that nothing was broken. Her knee was starting to feel a bit stiff, but she knew that she was very lucky that she wasn't injured worse. She stood up slowly and looked into her bags. Her purchases were fine, and she was so grateful. Sam reminded herself that she had to be more careful, but with MS, things like this were bound to happen.

Samantha sat in her car for a moment, and reached into the bag for her journal. On the first page, she wrote: Sam's Dreams and Goals. The second page is where she started her list: show work in Gina's gallery, show paintings in the cafe gallery, come up with items to sell in cafe gift shop, make business cards, and finally she put: keep painting. She knew she would be adding to it, and she smiled thinking of all the things she may be writing in there in the future. On the back of the last page, she wrote: "Gratitudes" and on the back of the next to last page she started her list: for being alive, for being an artist, for having a job, for an amazing future. She figured that if she wrote gratitudes from the last page towards the first and her dreams and goals the other way, if they met in the middle some day she will have lived a very full life.

When she arrived home, she got out of the car very carefully and was very mindful of her steps as she climbed the stairs. She wanted to paint and play with her new canvases and brushes, but she knew better. Sam unpacked everything and put it away, then she went into the bathroom and began filling the tub with warm water. She needed to clean all of her wounds and assess the damage. The hot bath hopefully would keep everything from being too stiff. Her knee was swelling a bit, but there was only a superficial scrape on it. Her wrist stung as she lowered it into the water, but she preferred to soak it a bit to scrubbing it right away. She found herself wishing she had poured a glass of wine prior to getting into the bath, but she would have to do without. Besides, the combination of a hot bath and a glass of wine was likely only in her past now, as she couldn't take the risk of falling.

Sam knew she would still have a glass of wine now and then, but she had to be more cautious and make better choices. She also realized that MS gave her a perfect excuse to never wear heels again, and that thrilled her! Sam hated the discomfort of heels, she felt like it was torture. Now she wouldn't have to ever wear them again, you know, for safety.

After her soak in the tub, Sam bandaged her hand, but she decided against any other treatments for her wounds. Her knee was swelling just a little, mostly around the little scrape on it, and it was clean, so she wiped a tiny bit of antiseptic ointment on it and let it be. She looked at her watch, deciding if there was any time to paint. Sam decided to paint the edges of the three remaining paintings with naked edges, and complete the signature on all of them. At some point, she hoped to reclaim her table to use it for meals again, but for now, it was quite handy to lay the paintings on it to finish them.

Samantha realized the paintings on the easels were completed and dry, so she removed those and put blank gessoed canvases on them. She did not have a lot of time, but was inspired to start a new painting. Samantha got out her palette and squeezed equal amounts of green and blue oil paints on them. She also poured a bit of gel medium between the colors. Sam used her palette knife to mix the two together in the middle, leaving some pure blue and pure green. She got her 3" brush out and put one end in the green and extended it out to the blue, with the middle half the mixed color. Sam swirled the brush around on the canvas, swirling, dipping, and swirling some more. She covered the edges with the mixed color and stepped back. Simple but gorgeous she decided. Sam signed the painting and it was complete. Every time she painted something that didn't take days, she was shocked, but she often loved these simple paintings the most.

Just before bed, Sam got her journal in it and flipped to her gratitude page. On it, she wrote: I'm grateful that I didn't buy the huge canvas today because I may have injured myself worse or broken the canvas if I had it with me. She sat her journal on her nightstand and turned her lamp off, smiling as she drifted off to sleep.

Chapter 37

Sam was thankful for working the early shift. It felt good with her natural body rhythms to work 6am-1pm. She always woke up early, no matter what time she went to bed, and she always faded in early afternoon. Samantha often found a second wind late afternoon, but mid day she just wanted to nap. That didn't work too well when you work the swing shift, or the graveyard shift for that matter. She corrected herself, when it's a care facility, you don't refer to it as a graveyard shift, you call it the noc shift, short for nocturnal.

During her break, Sam remembered working a noc shift last year. They had a resident named Joan who had been a noc shift RN her entire career. Joan was a night owl, there was no getting around that. The kitchen would make her plates during the day and leave them in the fridge. The noc shift would heat them up and take them to her, and she also received her baths during the night. Joan was the most difficult thing about working noc shift. She would use her pull cord to call the aids at least once per hour, often more, and she was never pleasant. Sam was thankful that she almost always slept through the morning shift.

Today, however, Joan was awake, and she was pulling her pullcord every few minutes. For the first part of her shift, Joan kept Samantha running, however, when Joan complained of a sore throat, Sam got the med aide on duty and then went to help other residents. She realized that for once, she was thankful to not be on meds. Samantha went to check the shower schedule and noticed that Connie was next. She headed upstairs to her room and knocked lightly as she used her key. As she entered the room, she saw Connie sitting on the floor, just in front of her couch. Sam rushed over to her.

"Connie, are you ok? What happened?" Samantha asked her, looking around where Connie was sitting. The coffee table was pushed away, but nothing else seemed out of place, and her legs didn't look injured.

"Oh my dear, I just went to sit on my couch and must have not got it right. I sat right on the edge, it seems, then just slid right off," Connie said as she chuckled, "it was almost like being on one of those slides, down I went, though I think the ride was much too short!"

"Oh Connie, I'm so glad you're alright! I do love your sense of adventure! It's time for your shower, during which we can make sure you don't have any injuries. Let me help you up, and while you catch your breath for a moment I will get everything ready for your shower. Are we washing your hair today?" Sam asked as she helped Connie to her feet.

"Oh, yes, I was wondering if you could help me set it too? I have my curlers all ready to go," Connie asked.

"You know I love to help with your hair, Connie! I will check on you right before I leave to see if it's dry enough to comb out, but if it's not, I'll leave a note for the next shift, alright?" Sam told her as she gathered up her towel, washcloth, and clothes.

As Sam helped Connie into the shower, she looked for bruises or scrapes from her sliding off of the couch. Thankfully she saw none. She held the shower head while Connie sat on the shower chair and washed herself, then she washed Connie's hair. Connie always smiled serenely as Sam scrubbed her scalp. After the shower, Sam helped her to dress and put Connie's hair in rollers for her. Connie was very particular and Sam was the only one besides the beautician and Gina who could fix her hair. Sam only recently was able to convince Connie that any of the staff was capable of combing it out for her.

"Alright, Connie, all done. Thank you for letting me help you today, and I'll check on you before I leave to see if your hair is dry. Would you like me to pop in before lunch to tie a scarf over it?" Sam asked her, remembering that Connie would not want to eat in the dining room without the curlers covered properly.

"Oh yes, dearie, thank you so much. I will wait for you before I head to lunch. And perhaps we can walk down together?" Connie said.

"I would love nothing more, I assure you!" Sam said as she headed to the door, "See you in awhile!"

Sam smiled at the thought of walking Connie to lunch. So often Connie chose to stay in her room, and Sam felt like it was because she was lonely, but today she would get to escort her to the dining room. Samantha chuckled as she realized how odd her reaction was. Well, odd for her. She loved the residents, but had always kept a healthy distance, except when it came to death or grief. During those times, Sam would comfort the residents, she would hold their hands, she always had tissues handy, and was always ready to listen to them reminisce about their loved one. On her break, Sam pondered this tendency, and she supposed it was due to losing her mother at such a young age. Grief and mourning were emotions that she understood. A new realization tugged at her while she thought about that. Wouldn't it be nice if she could now understand love and life? A tear rolled down her cheek as she realized it was time.

"Oh I'm sorry, I didn't mean to interrupt your break," Karen said as she walked in to the break room, "I mean, um, are you alright? You seem sad."

Karen had begun working at the assisted living shortly after Samantha did. Unlike Sam though, Karen had quickly become friends with many of her coworkers. In fact, Karen had often whispered about how cold Sam was.

"I'm alright. Just realizing that my life has been a bit misdirected, and until recently I haven't really been living," Sam replied, and realized that Karen's eyes were kind, so she continued, "my mom died when I was 14 and it hardened me. I lost my son just before starting this job and then my marriage. We were both so shocked when Jacob died and I withdrew even more. He couldn't reach me, and he had to mourn alone. That is so terrible. Now, after finding out that I'm dying, only now do I feel the urge to really live. Isn't that crazy?"

"You're dying?" Karen said, wide eyed.

"I was recently diagnosed with multiple sclerosis, which is what my mom also had. So yes, I'm dying, but I guess we all are, I just may be going a bit sooner, but I'm awake now if that makes sense," Samantha said.

"I'm so sorry for your diagnosis, Sam, but it almost seems like a gift," Karen said.

"Oh it is. I wish I had woken up sooner, but I feel like I have time to live my life still. I mean, some people never get the chance to turn things around right?" Sam responded, "oh my, look at the time! I'm going to walk Connie to lunch. Karen, it has been really nice talking to you and I hope we can do it again sometime."

"I've enjoyed it, thank you for opening up to me, Sam. It means a lot. I need to go get meds ready, I'll see you at lunch," she said as Sam headed out the door.

"Hey Connie, are you ready for me to put your scarf on you and take you to lunch?" Sam said as she walked into Connie's room.

"Hey there Sam, I've just about got her ready and I think I'm going to sit with her today, if that's alright," Gina said.

"That's awesome, Gina! As long as Connie doesn't mind," Sam said as she winked at Connie.

"Oh dear, I feel like a belle at a ball right now. You two are so kind to me. Thank you for coming to have lunch with your mother, Gina. And thank you, Sam for taking such good care of me. I love you both," Connie said.

Without even thinking, Sam went over and gave Connie a hug. While she did so, she realized that Connie is around the same age her mom would have been. Samantha knew that hugging her mom would feel like this.

"I'd better let you two get to lunch. I will see you down there," Sam said as she walked to the door, "I believe the choices today are chicken or salmon."

"Hey, Sam, can we talk after lunch? Will you have time for a break then?" Gina said as Samantha was walking out the door.

"Oh, absolutely, Gina. I took one break earlier, but I have a half hour lunch, is everything alright?" Sam asked.

"Oh Gina, don't keep her hanging like that. Sam, you are going to be a famous artist soon! And I plan to be at the party!" Connie blurted out.

"Mom! You couldn't keep a secret to save your life, could you?" Gina laughed "let's talk details during your lunch, alright, Sam?"

"Thank you so much, I look forward to it!" Sam said breathlessly. She felt like she was floating towards the dining room. As she tripped walking down the stairs she thought "I should have taken the elevator." Sam tumbled down an entire flight of stairs. Luckily she was empty handed and didn't try to stop her fall with her wrists. She imagined looking like a rag doll, flopping down, however it must have not sounded like a rag doll because Jack had heard the ruckus from his office and came running to her aid.

"Geez, Sam, are you alright?" Jack said, reaching for her, but not to help her up. She could see his eyes scanning her for injuries. She started moving slowly, so he could see that she is alright. Sam was amazed that nothing hurt very badly. The stairs were very well padded and there was nothing in her way, so it was a clear shot.

"I'm good, Jack! What score would you give that tumble? On a scale of 1-10?" Sam asked as she began to stand.

"Well, I'd say at least a 9.5 are you sure you're alright? What happened?" Jack asked, still obviously rattled.

"Jack, I'm alright, really. And it was all my fault. I should have taken the elevator, but I was so excited. I'm not that great on stairs these days but I wasn't thinking. You see, I went to walk Connie down for lunch, Gina was there and Connie blurted out that I was going to be showing my art at Gina's gallery, so I was kind of floating down, well, until I tumbled. I feel fine though, and wow, can you believe I'm going to show my art in a gallery?" Sam said, talking very quickly from her adrenaline rush.

"That doesn't surprise me a bit, Sam, I knew it would happen! Would you do me a favor though and let Sandra check you out before you serve lunch? I'll go get started for you while you see her," Jack said, walking towards the kitchen and pointing her to the med room.

Sam knocked on the partially open door as she approached. One of their residents, Mark was just getting up from getting his insulin shot and Samantha opened the door for him as she approached. He nodded as he walked by, already looking to see if his friends were in the dining room yet.

"What can I do for you, Sam?" Sandra asked.

"Jack is insisting you check me out before he'll let me serve lunch. I took a tumble down the stairs, and I'm not hurt, but he just wants to make sure," Samantha replied.

"Oh dear, did you trip on something?" Sandra asked her as she started looking her over.

"No," Sam said, chuckling, "in fact, I had just received amazing news and my mind was elsewhere, so I was kind of floating. I should have taken the elevator since I generally end up rolling down stairs these days. But I feel fine. I got up very slowly, Jack checked me over before I got up. Ankles and wrists seem to be fine, I'm not dizzy, and I don't hurt anywhere."

"You certainly seem fine to me. If you have any vision changes or headaches while you are at work, see me immediately. If it happens after work, go to the emergency department, alright?" Sandra instructed, "would you mind sharing this amazing news?"

"Oh yes! I am going to show my paintings in Gina's gallery! I don't have any details yet, but Connie blurted it out when I went to get her for lunch," Sam responded.

"Samantha, that is excellent news! Please keep me posted when you know the details, I would love to attend your big art show, and next time, take the elevator, would you?" Sandra said, winking at her then turned to check over the med-aide's work.

Sam went into the kitchen to relieve Jack, who was waiting for the orders for Mark's table. She grabbed an apron off the hook inside the door and put it on quickly.

"One chicken and two salmon please, and Mark wanted me to tell you that he loves your salmon" Jack said to Russ, the cook.

"Hey Jack, I'll take over. Sandra said all is fine, but if I get dizzy or start feeling bad to see her or go to the emergency department. But I am fine," Sam assured him.

"Alright, and when lunch is over, I hope you have some salmon for me, Russ, it looks great!," Jack said, taking off his apron, "glad you are alright, Sam!"

Sam carried the three plates to Mark's table and placed a salmon in front of Mark, "now who has the chicken?" she asked, and placed it in front of Jerry when he raised his hand, "alright then Jim, this other salmon must be yours. Is there anything else I can get you?"

Each of the gentlemen shook their head dismissively and Sam headed to Connie's table. She and Gina had sat over to the side by themselves. Connie's eyes were twinkling as she looked at Sam approaching.

"What can I get for you, ladies? Chicken or Salmon?" Sam asked as she approached.

"I would love the salmon, but mom has never liked seafood, so she will have the chicken," Gina told her.

"Oh honey, that's not true. I like shellfish, but not, well, fish fish..." Connie corrected her, laughing, "yes, I'd love the chicken, dear."

"One of each, Russ, for Connie and her daughter," Sam said as she went into the kitchen. She and Karen were a good team, never crowding Russ. It seemed every time Sam went in, Karen was going out. Russ wasn't much of a talker, but he was always nice to Sam. She had seen him blow up at some of the other aides, but she seemed to calm him and she was thankful for that. He handed her the two plates and she headed out the kitchen door, just as Karen was coming in. For the first time ever, Samantha and Karen smiled at each other in passing.

"Here you are, ladies. One salmon and one chicken. Enjoy your lunch!" Sam said as she put the plates in front of them, "is there anything else I can get you?"

"Can I get some coffee, dear? I'm afraid we came in after it was served," Connie said, pointing to her coffee cup.

"Oh, absolutely! Gina, what can I get you to drink?" Sam asked.

"I'd like some iced tea, please, no lemon," Gina replied.

Sam nodded and headed to the kitchen to get a glass of iced tea. She came to the table carrying that and the coffee pot.

"Here you go," she said as she set the tea in front of Gina and filled Connie's cup with coffee, "anything else for you two?"

"I think we are all set, thank you so much, Sam," Gina said as she reached for the sweetener for her tea.

"Enjoy!" Sam said, then looked around and noticed that everyone had food in front of them. She began going table to table to see if anyone needed anything. On days when salmon is a choice, there isn't much talking going on during lunch. It seemed to her that everyone was enjoying their meal. She grabbed a coffee pot and made a round around the dining room after signaling to Karen to go ahead and take her lunch now. Sam enjoyed the small talk around the tables. She loved seeing each resident's personality come through as they talked to their friends. Sam made her way, table by table, to make sure that everyone's needs were met. Then she went and got the dessert cart, today it was berry crisp. Russ outdid himself, Sam was thinking as she served everyone. One more round with the coffee pot and she could sit for awhile. She popped into the break room and took Karen dessert.

"Hey, you don't want to miss out on this!" Sam said as she put it on the table.

"I'm so full, but you're right, I don't want to miss that, thank you, Sam!" Karen said as she moved her plate out of the way and put her dessert in front of her. Sam grabbed her plate before Karen could argue.

"I'm headed to the kitchen anyway, enjoy your dessert!" Sam said as she left.

"Russ, the residents love their lunch and many asked me to thank you. So. Thank you for the fine meal, sir," Sam said with a curtsy.

Russ simply smiled and blushed. Samantha hadn't meant to embarrass him so she grabbed the bussing cart and took it out to the dining room. Many residents had already gotten up to leave so she started clearing their tables. The ones who were lingering had no objections to her clearing their dishes away. She knew that many would be staying for bingo, so she made sure there were tables set up for that, then she rolled the cart into the kitchen and began putting everything in the sink and loading up the dishwasher trays.

"Thanks for bringing me dessert, Sam! Hey Russ, amazing meal!" Karen said as she popped her head in to put her final dishes near the sink, "I'm going to see if anyone needs anything and go document meds. Enjoy your lunch!"

"Hey Sam, I made you a plate, and I'm going on break now. Enjoy your lunch," Russ said, heading for the back door.

"Thanks, Russ!" Sam hollered after him.

Sam really enjoyed washing dishes, even in this industrial setting. It was an easy task, you could see the results right away, and she often spent the time troubleshooting anything going on in her life. She realized she didn't have time to daydream today though because Gina wanted to talk with her. Her first gallery show! Sam couldn't stop smiling as she continued to wash the dishes.

"Hey Sam, I was just checking to see when you would be on lunch," Gina said, popping her head in to the kitchen.

"Just a couple more minutes, Gina and I'll be all done here. Since bingo is going on, how about we meet in the break room?" Sam replied.

"No worries, I'll watch the bingo game until you're done. Thanks for fitting me into your schedule!" Gina said and popped back out.

Samantha finished up the dishes and grabbed her plate. She walked by Russ' office and popped her head in before she left the kitchen, "thanks for lunch, Russ!"

He nodded towards her, but she was already gone. He heard the door swing shut behind her and knew he was not likely to see her again today.

"Hey, Gina, I'm all done now!" Sam whispered as she approached her. Gina followed her to the break room and began talking before Samantha even got seated.

"I'm really sorry about how you found out. Mom can't keep a secret, I swear. The gallery would be thrilled to show your work. When I spoke to my colleagues, it was unanimous!" Gina said breathlessly, "we would love to hang your work all next month, with a gathering so that your public can meet the esteemed artist. What do you think about that?"

"Gina, I don't even know what to say," Sam said, thinking how odd it felt to be speechless.

"Here's my card, I'm going to let you eat now in peace. Let's talk about this, and I will arrange transport of your art to the gallery," Gina said, and was quickly gone.

Samantha shook her head, wondering what just happened. She had gone from cold and isolated to feeling alive and energized. She laughed out loud when she realized that her turning point was being diagnosed with multiple sclerosis. Sam was ready to throw in the towel, had given up on her marriage, was living in a self imposed hell, and yet being diagnosed with a terminal illness is what snapped her out of it.

She had begun attending the support group meetings that the MS Society sponsored, and Sam knew that she was lucky. She was very fortunate to have been diagnosed when she did, lucky to have the type of MS that she had, and that she could still work. Samantha had her off days, when she was dizzy, or her foot drop was especially bad, but so far her good days far outnumbered her bad.

Chapter 38

After lunch, Sam decided to check in on Connie, she was touched that Connie had been so excited for her. She thought of all that she needed to do before her show. She needed to go over each of her paintings and make sure that the edges are painted and they are signed. Sam shook her head, smiling because she knew she has checked that a dozen times. She was so thankful that Gina had said she would transport the art because she had tied the large canvas on top of her car when she bought it and had no idea how she would get it to the gallery. If all went well, that one would sell and transporting it back would become someone elses problem.

She knocked gently on Connie's door, hoping she wasn't napping. All she heard was a muffled sound, so she entered. Samantha had a bad feeling.

"Connie, are you alright?" Sam said upon entering. She scanned the room. Connie was sitting on the floor again, in front of her couch, and seemed unable to get up. It looked like she had been trying to turn so she could get on her knees and pull herself up onto her couch. She looked exhausted and Sam rushed over to her, looking for signs of injury as she went.

"Oh, I'm fine, dear. I just slipped off my couch and couldn't reach my pull cord. I feel like such a bother sometime!" Connie responded.

"Does it hurt anywhere, Connie? Can you wiggle your fingers and toes for me?" Sam requested.

"No, no pain," Connie said, moving her fingers and toes as Samantha requested.

"Good, now can you wiggle your nose?" Sam said, laughing.

"Oh you silly girl! How about you help me up and onto the couch?" Connie asked.

"Alright, I'm satisfied that you aren't broken, Connie. Put your arms around my neck and I'm going to put my feet between your legs here. That's right, just hold on, dear," Samantha talked Connie through each step until she was back on the couch, and once Connie was situated, Sam sat next to her, "now, let's figure out how that happened and make sure it doesn't happen again, shall we?"

"I went to sit and I guess I wasn't back far enough, so I just slid onto the floor," Connie said.

"Alright. Do you remember when you had met with the physical therapist, Connie? It's important to always make sure that you feel the couch or the bed with the back of your legs before sitting. So that's one thing that can be done differently. But let's say you do slide off again. How can we make sure you are able to call for help? I can extend the pull cord so that you can reach it all the way down to the floor. Will that help?" Samantha asked her.

"Oh yes, dear. I was just about to call 911, but I felt like that would be a little silly, really. When you call 911 the firetruck and the ambulance show up and that seems to be unnecessary for one little old lady who slid off of her couch," Connie said, chuckling.

"So you had your phone nearby?" Samantha asked her.

"Oh yes, dear, I almost always have it with me on my walker, plus I have another on my nightstand and one on my end table. I think it's overkill but Gina insisted that I always have one nearby," Connie said, shaking her head.

"Gina is a very smart woman, Connie. And I have a suggestion. What if I program the facilities phone number into your phone so that if this does happen again you can call the office. Jack may answer, it may be one of the aides, but someone will be sent up to help. Does that sound like it will work for you?" Samantha asked her.

"Oh yes, that sounds lovely, dear. Gina programmed her number. When I press number one, she answers. So it can't be one. Let's make the facility number five. Right in the middle of the number pad, and my favorite number so it will be easy to remember," Connie said.

"Alright, it's programmed in. I am going to make you a couple signs to remind you, just until it becomes something you can do without a thought. I will also put in your chart so that everyone is aware and I will let Gina know too. I'm sure she'll appreciate that you have a way of contacting us," Sam told her, writing a couple notes to place near the phones to remind Connie. She also taped one on her wall, "I know these are ugly, and we'll remove them as soon as it's not so new, ok?"

"Oh dear, I'm not worried about how it looks, I appreciate you helping me. I'm glad it was you who found me, Sam. No one else would have taken this much time with me. You are my favorite, but don't tell anyone else that," Connie said, chuckling again.

"Thank you Connie, you are my favorite too, and I don't care who knows! Would you mind if I gave Gina a call now to let her know what happened, that you are alright, and that we created a plan?" Samantha asked her.

"Wonderful idea, dear, sometimes I mix up my words and I don't want to alarm her. She does worry about me, that girl," Connie said to her while Sam dialed. Samantha very calmly told Gina what had happened, how her mom had slid onto the floor.

"Oh no! Is she alright?" Gina said, sounding panicked.

"She is perfectly fine, Gina, no injuries at all, and she is very calm. I helped her up and checked her out. I will have

Sandra check on her as well. However, I reminded her about feeling the couch or bed on the backs of her legs before sitting. I also am putting in a work order to extend her pull cord so she can reach it even from the floor, and I programmed the facility phone number as number five on her phone so she has us on speed dial. Also, to help her remember, I put up a few notes around her apartment. Is there anything else you can think of for me to do?" Sam asked.

"Wow, Sam, it certainly sounds like you have thought of everything. Thank you so much, and thank you for letting me know. Please let Sandra know that I'm available if she notices anything that I need to make an appointment for, but if I don't hear from her, I will assume all is well. You have put my mind at ease, Sam, thank you so much!" Gina said.

"Anytime, Gina! I will be contacting you soon about the show, but I need to go for now so I can talk with Sandra and do some charting, have a great day," Sam said before hanging up the phone.

"Connie, I'm going to go talk to Sandra and she will be coming up to check on you at some point, just so you know. I'm certain there are no injuries, but it's always good to get a second opinion," Sam said to Connie, winking as she did so.

"That sounds good, dear, and it will give me a chance to brag on you to her! You know I will be at the gallery for your show too. You are going to be famous, and hopefully won't forget about us little people," Connie said with a chuckle as she put her hand on Sam's.

"I'd never forget you, Connie! And I'm thrilled that you will be there! It's like a dream come true, actually, a dream I had been afraid to hope for," Sam said to Connie, who was nodding, "however, there's lots to do before then, like talking to

Sandra! I will see you soon, and Sandra will be up to check up on you. Have a good rest of the day!"

As Sam waited for the elevator, she realized how fortuitous it was that she went to Connie's room when she did. She had the gift of good timing more often than not, she thought to herself. With Rodney her timing was good enough to find him, but unfortunately not good enough to save him, Samantha thought, frowning, but his suffering could have prolonged had she not walked by when she did. She was just thankful that nothing bad had happened for Connie.

"Hey Sandra, can I talk to you a minute?" Sam said, as she approached the med room, noting the door was open and Sandra was sitting at her desk.

"Of course, what's up, Sam? Is this about your show?" Sandra asked.

"Oh, well, I will have a show next month, but it's not about that. I promise to get you more details about that soon, but I wanted to talk to you about Connie," Sam responded.

"What's going on with Connie?" Sandra said, alarmed.

Sam told her everything that had occurred, including the call to Gina and programming the number into the phone, "I also told her that you would check her out, Sandra, just as a precaution. I'm sure she's ok, but it would put her and Gina's mind at ease if you would double check. Gina also wanted you to know she's available if Connie needs to be seen by a doctor but she will assume all is well if she doesn't hear from you."

"As always, Sam, great job. You seemed to cover all the bases and I will check on Connie in just a few minutes. I'm glad you stopped in on her when you did," Sandra said.

"Yes, so am I. I'm almost off, but will you let me know if there is anything I missed with her? I mean, if there are any issues? It would mean a lot to me," Sam replied, pleadingly.

"If there is anything life threatening, I will, but if I see a scratch or a bruise, no. You will be back tomorrow and can see her then, deal?" Sandra compromised.

"That sounds alright, Sandra, thank you. I need to go do my charting before I'm off," Sam said, heading out the door.

Chapter 39

Sam woke with a start, realizing that her show is one week away. The van would be coming today to pick up her work. She had been having nightmares all night, that the canvases broke on the way to the show, that the van crashed in a fiery ball on the way to the gallery, and finally that there was some paint cans in the van and that crashed and as it rolled the paint got spilled all over her work.

"Okay, Sam, breathe, these are professionals and all will go well," she told herself as she sat up in bed. Samantha looked at the clock, "it's only 7:30, they will be here around 10. Time for some breakfast!"

She had some steak left over from dinner a couple of nights ago. Sam had purposefully saved it for this morning, she wanted every part of today to be special. Her steak paired beautifully with some eggs perfectly cooked, her favorite way, over medium. She had bought some fresh squeezed orange juice at the farmers market on the weekend and it tasted like sunshine to her on this promising morning. Sam savored every bite of her breakfast, and thought about all the things she is grateful for as she did so. She began listing them: her creativity, her job, her health (she knew it could be so much worse, and sometimes it was, but overall she was doing great), her failed marriage for all it taught her, MS for teaching her to embrace each moment, the promise of her art show, and the future with her new outlook on life.

Sam looked at the clock on the microwave. She was surprised to see it was 9:30 already, she realized she didn't have much time so she hopped in the shower, thankful that she had washed her hair last night. She was pleased to note that her shower took less than ten minutes as she rushed to get dressed.

Sam brushed her hair, and put on mascara and a light coating of lipstick. She was pleased with how she looked today, she seemed to be glowing, not only did she look like she was glowing but she felt like she was, Samantha couldn't stop smiling.

Sam had cleaned the house last night and arranged the art in her living room. Gina's assistant had told her the van would be here at ten, they would wrap her work individually and load it, then they would unload it at the gallery. Inventory would be taken and signed by her on each end, so after the van was done at her apartment, she had a little bit of time before going to the gallery and seeing all of her work there. Sam had put the title on the back of each work and already had her own inventory, of course, so it should all go smoothly. She loaded the dishwasher with her breakfast dishes and started it just as she heard a knock on the door.

"Come on in!" Sam said as she opened the door to two young men, "I have everything ready right here in the living room. If you have any questions, please let me know."

"Ma'am, I'm Joe and this is Connor. We've been doing this awhile and you are in good hands. Did the gallery tell you what to expect?" Joe asked.

"Yes, they said you would wrap up my work and load it in the van, inventorying everything as you went. I'll sign off on it here, then I'll check the gallery to make sure that all the work is safe there, is that basically all?" Samantha asked.

"Yes, ma'am, how many works do you have?" Joe asked.

"I have 37, and the title of each one is on the back. I have an extra copy of my inventory if it will help you," Sam replied.

"Oh, that would be great, then we will start wrapping them up and get them loaded. Can we prop the door open without any fear of pets getting out?" Joe asked.

"Oh, I don't have any pets, so no worries of that," Sam said, "I will get out of your way, let me know if you need anything, and if you two get thirsty, there is some lemonade in the refrigerator."

Sam went into her room, leaving the door open of course, and started folding laundry. It was killing her to not be in there orchestrating everything, but these guys were professionals and she knew that it was best if she stayed out of their way. She did keep checking though, just to make sure they didn't need her. However, once she saw the care they were putting into their job she relaxed some. It took them about an hour and a half to get everything wrapped and placed in the van.

"We're all done, ma'am. Everything should be unloaded and unwrapped in two hours time at the latest, and that's including drive time. There's no rush, but we will need you to sign off on it and double check that everything is there and in excellent shape," Joe said to Sam as he walked towards the door.

"I will be there within two hours then and thank you both for everything. You both set my mind at ease," Sam replied, extending her hand to shake each of theirs.

Samantha knew that if she left right away she would just have to wait at the gallery, so she busied herself with cleaning. It was the first time since she started painting again that almost all of the canvasses were out of her apartment, she realized that now is the best time to clean up her supplies and her painting area. She made a mental note to buy extra drop cloths, then decided it would be best to take inventory and make a shopping list as she cleaned. She had all but exhausted her supply of gel medium, gesso, and many colors of her paints. Samantha inspected her brushes, which were all in very good shape, but she put brush conditioner on the list. She also made a note to look for some texturing tools for a new direction she would like to explore.

Once her painting area was tidied up, Sam unloaded the dishwasher and made a salad for herself for lunch. She smiled as she got out all of the ingredients: grilled and diced chicken, blue cheese, bell pepper, cucumber, spinach, brocolli, snow peas, ranch dressing, and some sunflower kernels. Samantha had recently begun a gratitude practice, where she would write down five things she was thankful for in her journal before bed. That practice made her take notice throughout the day and as she sat down to eat she began listing off all of the things she was thankful for. Her list always included her job, her health, her creativity, today she added the gallery, her apartment, this beautiful and filling salad… Sam was filled with joy while she ate.

Never one to leave a mess, Sam loaded her dishes into the dishwasher and gathered up the garbage before she headed to the gallery. Looking at her watch she realized she may still be a little bit early, but she was now anxious to get there. She grabbed her camera and inventory on the way out the door.

"Sam! Isn't this all so exciting?" Gina asked her, hugging her.

"I can't begin to thank you, Gina, I'm so honored to even be here," Sam replied.

"Oh now, we are blessed to have your work here, and I feel like this is the beginning of a beautiful relationship," Gina said as she led Sam into the main gallery, "let's check the inventory, make sure everything arrived beautifully, then discuss placement, shall we? Do you need anything before we begin? Water? Lunch?"

"I just ate, actually, and I'm alright on the water for now, thank you," Sam replied.

"Well, don't hesitate to ask if you need anything, you are a very important person around here and we want to keep you happy! What I need you to do is look over every single piece of art, check it off on the inventory, and inspect it for any damage, I will leave you alone because it will take you awhile and you don't need me distracting you. If you need me though, I'll be in my office, through that door right over there," Gina said, pointing to her office door, easily recognizable because it had her name plaque on it. Sam nodded and got her inventory out. She walked over to the first painting and noticed Gina was already gone. Once again, she was alone with her art, Sam smiled as she realized there was no place she'd rather be.

Samantha did exactly as Gina asked, checking each item off of the inventory, and noting the condition. She found no damage on any of her paintings and was so thankful that she was working with professionals. Just as she was completing her tasks, Gina re-appeared.

"All done with that part, Sam?" Gina asked.

"Yes, every piece is here, in pristine shape. I'm so thankful that your crew has taken such care, Gina," Sam gushed to her.

"Believe me, it's our pleasure, Sam. Would you like something before we talk about placement?" Gina asked her.

"If you don't mind, Gina, can I take a little bit of a break? I brought a protein bar and think I should probably sit down a bit, I'm feeling a little weak. I run out of steam a lot quicker than I used to," Sam replied.

"Of course, let's go into the break room and I'll grab you a water. It will be nice to relax for a little while, and if you need to take breaks at any point, just let me know, alright?" Gina said, looking into Sam's eyes. Sam could sense compassion, and a bit of worry.

"I will let you know, Gina, thank you. I'm very fortunate that my MS isn't worse than it is, really. I do try hard to keep it in check though. And just so you know, things that will make me worse are temperature variations, stress, hunger, things like that. I've learned some tricks though, like layering my clothes so I can adjust, carrying snacks with me, and some breathing techniques when things get stressful. So I'm very good at managing it all myself, but if you see me stumble or if I slur my words, you may want to get me a chair, alright? It's rarely a problem, but I have no way of knowing what this whole gallery showing will bring, you know?" Sam asked her.

"Thank you for letting me know what to look for, Sam. I don't want to mother you, but I really do appreciate you explaining it to me. If you don't mind, I will fill some of the staff in on the things to look for as well, so that if anything goes wrong we can make it as smooth as possible, would that be alright?" Gina responded to her.

"I have an idea, how about if we have a little meeting before the show and I can tell them myself? That way they can see for themselves that I am capable, but I can also explain some things about my disease, does that seem fair to you?" Sam asked.

"That's a beautiful idea, Sam, thank you so much for offering to do that. I admire how you live your life, I have to tell you," Gina replied.

Sam could feel herself blushing, but when she turned to comment, Gina was gone. Sam smiled as she finished her protein bar and her bottle of water. She knew that when she was ready Gina would be in her office and would be willing to come out and talk to her about where everything will be placed before the show. Sam took a deep breath before getting up, grateful to be here.

"Hey Gina?" Sam said, knocking on Gina's office door.

"Come on in, Sam! Are you ready to help me decide where to hang everything?" Gina said as Sam entered.

"I am, Gina, and I also wanted to thank you again. Your guys treated my work with such care. It's all here and it's in great shape. I'm so thankful," Sam said as Gina got up, they walked out into the gallery together.

"It's my pleasure, Sam, absolutely my pleasure. I feel the same way every time I visit my mom, you know. You approaching me that day was completely fortuitous. I'm so glad you did, and this show is going to be amazing, I just know it. I thought we would start with your largest painting, what is it, 6'x5'? I peeked earlier and I must tell you it is gorgeous! Those words seem so perfect for your show, and I wanted to use it in the brochures if you don't mind. Samantha Green, It's Good to be Alive Gallery Show, what do you think?" Gina asked.

"That sounds perfect, Gina. I'm not sure how you did that, but that one painting, with the words that you suggested, embodies all that I feel and the way I'm trying to live my life. Will that painting be the focal point then? Were you thinking this center wall that you see as you walk in the door?" Sam asked her, walking over to the wall as she did.

"Are you sure you weren't a gallery owner in a past life, Sam?" Gina chided her, "that is precisely what I was thinking, and I do think that if that is the first thing that every single person sees when they walk in that they will then be drawn in and want to see every single piece of your art, and even though

174

you have a large number of paintings, my prediction is that the public will love it so much that they will leave wanting more. Of course, if you want to hear another prediction, I think many of them will fall so deeply in love with your work that they won't leave without taking some of it home."

"Gina, that would be a dream come true, I can assure you!" Sam replied, blushing.

"That reminds me, we need to talk pricing. Since this is your first show, your prices won't be as high as they will be someday. Do you have prices in mind for your work?" Gina asked.

"No, honestly I haven't even thought about it," Sam admitted.

"Well, if it's alright with you, I will have you talk with Patricia, she is our pricing expert, and she will help you get everything priced," Gina offered.

"That would be great, every time I feel like I'm in way over my head, you are prepared to help me out. Thank you so much!" Sam replied.

"It's not our first rodeo, Sam," Gina said with a wink, "and we love to help new artists get their start. If we didn't help with some of the steps, we fear it would be too overwhelming."

"Do you know when Patricia would be available? I can be here tomorrow afternoon. I work until noon but should be able to come after, but after 3 would really work better if that's possible," Sam said.

"I will have her check with you before you leave. I just have a few more questions about placement and I'll be done with you for the day. When you come back everything will be hung and Patricia will help you with pricing then we will get them all labeled," Gina responded.

Chapter 40

By the time Sam left she knew where everything would be hung and had a good idea of how things would look. She felt like she was walking on clouds as she left the gallery, until she turned the corner to go to the back parking lot and walked right into a gentleman and fell backwards, landing on her backside.

"Oh, excuse me, miss, I'm so sorry," he said as he reached out to help her up, "are you alright?"

"Yes, I'm alright. It was my fault. I was off in dreamland and wasn't paying attention to where I was going," Sam said, reaching out for his hand.

"My name is Zack, and at times I'm the world's clumsiest man, nice to meet you," he replied as he pulled her to her feet.

"I assure you the fault was mine, and no harm was done, I'm Sam, uh... Samantha, by the way," Sam attempted to reassure him.

"Samantha, I would love to make it up to you, perhaps over dinner, what do you say?" Zack asked.

"Um, well, that would be lovely, but the next couple weeks are so busy for me, with work, and getting ready for my exhibit," Sam stammered.

"Your exhibit?" he replied.

"Yeah, I paint, all my work will be on exhibit soon, that's why I'm here, actually, to help them decide where to hang everything," Sam said.

"Well tell me this, Samantha, will there be an evening when everyone can meet the artist? A black tie affair?" Zack inquired.

"Yes, it's in about two weeks, so that's why I'm so busy, so much going on," Sam said.

Zack reached into his jacket pocket and handed her his card, it simply said Zack Adams, Esq. and listed his cell number on it.

"What if I took you to a celebratory dinner prior to your opening?" Zack said.

"That should be alright, but I can't really commit right this minute," Samantha replied.

"You have my number, I hope you will use it," he said, bowing slightly before turning and walking away.

Sam watched him walk away for a moment. He was impeccably dressed in a slate grey pinstripe suit. Her intuition told her that if she looked at the label it would have a famous designer's name on it. He moved effortlessly, his back straight, his shoulders back. He had some grey hair near his temples, and aside from that, his hair was a deep brown color. She had also noticed his eyes, they were the color blue that she had seen in photos of the water around the Fiji Islands. He was a mystery, Zack Adams, Esq. Sam wondered if she would ever see him again. She tucked his card into her purse, remembering that she hadn't eaten since her granola bar.

As she got into her car, she tried to remember what she had at home for dinner. She decided as she drove that she would have a bowl of cereal and relax in the bath. It was still early enough that she could watch a movie after her bath if she chose. Sam knew she would need to get up for the early shift tomorrow, but her laundry was done, all dishes were clean, oh, she did need to unload the dishwasher she remembered.

When she got home, she thought it felt empty without all of her artwork. Sam realized that those paintings were like her children, her family. She birthed them, they lived here, and now they were all at the gallery. Sam felt lonely without them. She poured a bowl of cereal and went into the bathroom to fill the tub. She sat her bowl on the counter while she undressed and checked the water temperature, knowing that she couldn't handle it too hot, not with MS. If she submerged herself in too hot of a bath she would weaken and be unable to get out until after draining the tub, but by that point she would have cooled off and gotten a chill, adding to her difficulty. Once the temperature was perfect, she put the bowl on the edge of the tub and lowered herself into the water.

Sam remembered that just prior to being diagnosed, she took an extremely hot bath. So hot that it fogged up the entire bathroom and she was sweating as she bathed. Oh how she loved baths like that, until one day she got really tired in this bath, and couldn't raise herself out of it. She panicked and spent an extra hour in the tub, crying, not knowing of anyone who could help her. By the time she got out of the tub, she was shivering so much that her teeth were chattering.

While she soaked in the tub, she enjoyed her bowl of cereal, relishing every single bite, and then she tilted the bowl up, drinking down all the milk, dribbling some down her chin as she did so. As she wiped it off, she thought about Zack Adams, Esq. She thought of the view as he walked away. He certainly was handsome. She wondered if she should call him in a few days, or maybe even a week. Sam wished she knew what all the right protocol was, she wished she knew how to talk to someone she was interested in, how to show interest, how to make small talk, how to flirt, in fact, all the things involved in having a relationship. She knew that person would have been her mom, but she had missed out on all that a mom would have done for her. A mom would have instilled a sense of security in her, and made her know that someone out there loved her no matter what. Samantha felt a sadness wash over her and decided it was time to redirect her thoughts.

She began a mental to do list. Tomorrow at 4 pm, she would meet with Patricia and work on pricing. Sometime in the next few days she would need to go buy a dress and shoes for her big night, and she needed to decide what to do about Mr. Adams. As she dried off she found herself picturing him again. Those eyes, she could imagine drowning in them. Suddenly she felt silly. He was at an art gallery, perhaps he was part of Gina's team, or simply a collector. With these new thoughts swirling in her head, she had no idea how to proceed. Perhaps she would see if Gina knew him and go from there. As she put her robe on, she realized that she didn't want to watch a movie, she wanted nothing more than to paint. Smiling, she tossed her robe off and put her painting shirt on. She had found it at a thrift store, it was a man's dress shirt, size XXL and went almost to her knees.

Sam had three canvases left in her apartment, two of which had been gessoed and were sitting on the easels. She reached for the purple, and the yellow. She layered the colors on the canvas, just making horizontal stripes across it. She then used a clean, dry brush to blend between the lines, barely blending the two colors together, an effect that seemed to create an ethereal effect. She was happy with it so she moved to the other canvas.

On this one she chose a blue, the same color as the waters around Fiji, and yes, Zack Adams' eyes. She swirled it with some light grey and some white, swirling in about 3" diameters all over the entire canvas, blending lightly as she went.

"Oh, Sam, you've got it bad," she said to herself as she stood back to assess the painting. She stepped forward to blend a bit more. She smiled as she realized that she automatically painted the edges of her canvases this time. Sam looked at her watch and was surprised by how late it was. She signed the paintings and headed to bed.

Chapter 41

Samantha looked around, noticing details as she walked into the front door of work. Jack's office door was ajar, as usual, Marvin was reading the newspaper on the couch in the foyer, and Beatrice was snoozing in a chair. She breathed a sigh of relief, noting that all seemed well. Jack looked up and saw her, beckoning her into his office.

"Good morning, Jack!" Samantha said as she walked in.

"Hey there, Sam, I just wanted to let you know that your vacation was approved, and unless you don't like the idea, we've arranged to bus some of our residents to the show. Gina was going to take Connie, and I know there are a few others who wanted to go," Jack said.

"Oh Jack, thank you! I love that idea. And thank you for approving my vacation. I plan to get a lot of rest the day before my show, in hopes that I'm not too stressed or exhausted to enjoy it. Trying to stave off a MS flare up, you know?" Sam replied.

"Yes, and I think that's wise. I am excited to go to your show, as is my wife. We can say we knew you when," Jack said, smiling, "you'd better get to work, your public awaits."

Sam walked out of his office, laughing. Her public, indeed. Her public lived in an assisted living and needed help with showers, and she would have it no other way. Sam realized that this was her family. All of those years of shutting herself off and much of the time they were right here, waiting for her to let them in. She was thrilled some would be at her show, she thought as she made a mental note to ensure that the gallery was prepared to host them.

Sam stopped in the break room to talk to Karen and look at the shower list before gathering residents for breakfast.

She remembered the rocky start she and Karen had, and was thankful that they had moved beyond that and become friends now. Well, work friends, but Sam wanted to change that.

"Hey Karen, would you like to come over sometime, maybe have dinner at my place? Or I know of this awesome cafe we could go to," Sam said as Karen looked at the newspaper.

"Hey there! I would love to! How about we plan a night soon, order a pizza and watch a movie? That would be fun I think," Karen replied

"My show is in a week, and today is really busy but after that the only thing I have to do is shop for a dress, so I can do it anytime you'd like. I'm dreading shopping, but really looking forward to a relaxing night, so I'll just plan the shopping around it," Sam said.

"My sister owns a boutique," Karen said with a twinkle in her eye, "I'd love to help you pick out a dress if you want, I have been told I have a gift."

"I'm certainly not turning down that offer!" Samantha replied with a chuckle, "today is a no go, and I think tomorrow may be a rest day for me, but are you free the day after?"

"I am, it's my day off!" Karen said, "my sister's boutique opens at ten, so how about we get a dress picked out then do lunch at that cafe, and plan from there?"

"That sounds perfect!" Sam told her, "ok, I'm going to get everyone down for breakfast, see you later!"

Chapter 42

Patricia walked into the gallery at precisely four o'clock. Sam respected punctuality, she always liked to start things in a timely manner. In fact, she realized that she was very anxious when things did not start on time. Patricia was holding a notebook and they went from piece to piece, talking about the process and what each one meant to Sam as she painted it.

Patricia asked the question that Samantha expected: how long did this take you to paint? But she also wanted to know the supplies needed, the inspiration, the tools, and on some Patricia even asked her mood as she painted it. Afterwards, they sat in a conference room.

"Tell me why you paint, Sam," Patricia said.

"I paint because it saves me," Sam began, "my son, Jacob, was stillborn when I was almost eight months along, I withdrew and almost lost myself. Prior to that, my mom had died from MS when I was a teen, and I have always had a really hard time opening up to people. I started painting after Jacob's death, it brought a little color back into my world, but then I stopped for awhile, my marriage ended, and I was diagnosed with MS. I knew at that point that I had wasted my entire life, always building up barriers, and it was now time to live. I began painting again, and this time I really dove in. I have started living, the color has returned to my world. I paint because it saves me, every day."

"Wow, Sam, that's quite a story, I do hope you've told Gina all of that so she can put it in the brochure?" Patricia asked.

"Oh yes, we've discussed it. I am so thankful to know Gina, she has really opened doors for me!" Sam said.

"Gina is wonderful, as is everyone here, and after seeing your work, I can tell you this will be the first of many gallery shows for you. If that is what you want, anyway, your work is good enough that it will take you wherever you want it to. That being said, let's talk about pricing because I imagine many of these paintings are going to get snagged up!" Patricia said, smiling.

"That would be a dream come true!" Sam exclaimed, "I can put some money away so that when I have flare ups it's not such a financial worry."

"That is a great plan, Sam. I have a lot of ideas for price points based on many different factors, would you like to go over them individually or would you rather I move forward and work my magic? Either way is fine by me, but I'd like to let you know that I've been doing this for ten years now," Patricia said.

"I would be honored if you would go ahead and set the pricing. That would take a huge load off of my shoulders. And considering that task done, all that's left is for me to talk to all the staff prior to my show and I need to get a dress, maybe I should trade you tasks," Sam said with a chuckle.

Patricia laughed, "oh no, I can price art all day long, but I despise trying on clothes! Good luck with that, and I will see you at your show!"

Chapter 43

Sam stopped at her favorite store and made herself a salad to take home. She smiled as she realized that this store's salad bar has gotten her through so much in her life. Though she had tried many salad dressings in her life, the world's best balsamic vinaigrette was here. She filled her clear plastic container with spring greens, some grilled steak, sunflower seeds, pepperoncinis, bacon, broccoli, cauliflower, feta cheese, and blue cheese. She also filled a small round container with her salad dressing, put a lid on it and set it inside. Samantha was salivating at the thought of eating this salad, but wanted to do so while relaxing at home.

When she arrived home, there was a box in front of her door. It was addressed to her in beautiful, flowing letters, and where the return address should have been it simply said Cathy. Sam felt a little uneasy about opening this package, she hasn't known anyone named Cathy since she was extremely young. They had a neighbor named Cathy, but it was inconceivable that she would be hearing from her, there was no reason. She tossed the package onto the couch and plated her salad.

Sam put her plate on the table, poured a glass of iced tea, and then picked up the package, inspecting it. She didn't know what it was, who it was from, Samantha wondered if she should be opening it, but her instincts said it would be ok. Sam carried it into the kitchen and cut the tape with a knife, then sat down at the table with it. The first thing she saw was a handwritten letter with her name on it. She skimmed over it and discovered it was indeed the Cathy from her childhood. Cathy and her husband had been next door neighbors to her grandparents and had been friends with her mom. The letter went on to explain that when her mom was diagnosed she gave some things to Cathy for safekeeping and they were now being returned to Samantha.

Samantha sat the letter down and closed her eyes. She appreciated this moment as one of those "point of no return" moments. Sam sat still for a few minutes and took several deep breaths. Her curiosity, and her desire to have something tangible from her mother, won out. Sam reached into the box.

She pulled out a stack of photos. Her mother looked so young and vibrant in them, some from her high school days, and several others throughout her pregnancy and finally when she was bedridden. Sam sat them gently on the table then reached up to wipe a tear off of her cheek.

Also in the box was a journal. The cover was a deep, weathered brown leather with her mom's initials embossed on the cover, along with a sunrise image. She held it close to her face and inhaled. It smelled a little musty, but then she realized it smelled familiar. Like gardenias, and the memories washed over her. Her mom dressing up to go to church when she was very young, Sam watching her mom's every movement, wanting to play in her makeup, walking around in her mom's heels. Sam remembered her mom spraying gardenia perfume on herself and then onto Samantha as they giggled.

Sam looked down, noticing her salad and considered just pushing it aside, but knew that she really needed to eat even if she had to force herself to. Thankfully, she had gotten the world's best salad, so it looked appetizing. She decided she would look through the journal after eating, choosing to take the time to savor it.

The salad was delicious, she thought as she picked up Cathy's letter again. Sam was overcome with gratitude that this woman mailed this box to her after all these years. She wondered how she could get in touch with her, then noticed a

186

return address on the back of the envelope with the letter. Sam vowed to write to her tomorrow to express her appreciation.

Samantha always read magazines from the back cover to the front, and so now, without even thinking, she flipped to the back of the journal.

Dearest Sam,

Life sometimes takes some turns that we don't understand, but know, dear daughter, that everything happens for a reason. I have no understanding of why I should be taken from you, but I know that you are going to do great things in this world, things that you may not have been able to do if you had had an "easy" or "uneventful" life. Challenges give us wisdom, young one, and by the time you read this, I have no doubt that you will have plenty of wisdom to share.

I would give anything to see you grow, to attend your wedding, to hold my grandbabies, but that is not in the cards for me. I have advice anyway, and know that I'm always with you. First of all, Sammi, be kind, always be kind because you don't know what struggles others have. Next, be helpful, always reach a hand out when you see someone in need. That will fill your heart in ways that you could never imagine. Third, always live your life in color. Rich, vibrant color, no black and white, no grey. Be open to love, see the beauty, and really live, my gorgeous girl.

Don't forget that your mom loves you more than anything in the world. Also, don't forget to let love in, let it fill your heart, let it overflow. Promise me beautiful girl, promise me to let the love overflow.

Love, Mom

Sam sobbed as she finished the letter. Her heart was aching, she wanted so badly for her mom to hold her, to pat her hair as she used to do, to whisper "everything will be ok" while she rocked her. She caught her breath, wiped a tear and decided that she must get in touch with Cathy, and Samantha felt like she had to talk to her right this minute. Sam had no issues finding Cathy's phone number online. She was thankful that Cathy was still in her hometown. Her hands were shaking as she dialed the number.

"Hello?" a woman answered.

"Hi, is this Cathy?" Sam asked.

"It is. Who is asking, please?" Cathy asked.

"Oh, please forgive my lack of manners. This is Samantha Green," Sam replied.

"Oh dear, Sammi," Cathy said, "did you receive the box I mailed, dear?"

"Yes, ma'am, that's why I'm calling. I wanted to thank you for sending it to me, for finding me and for taking the time to get it to me. You have no idea what it means to me," Sam said.

"You're quite welcome, dear. Your mom and I were friends, we talked a lot. I have been looking for you for awhile. Are you married?" Cathy responded.

"No, unfortunately, I'm divorced. I'm a caregiver at an assisted living facility, I'm an artist, and I'm having a gallery show soon, do you think you could come for it?" Sam asked.

"Well, when is it dear?" Cathy replied, "I would love to see that, see what Barbara's daughter has done with her life."

"It's in about a week and a half, and I can sleep on the couch and you could stay here if you'd like, the show will likely be a late night," Sam said.

"Oh, I'd love to come to show, dear, but I can stay at a hotel. I do love hotels, they make me feel fancy. But perhaps I can come a little early for some catching up?" Cathy answered.

"That would be amazing. Thank you for sending the box, thank you for everything," Sam said, "I can't wait to see you. I will mail you the invitation, if that's alright."

"Absolutely dear, that would be wonderful. Tell me, do you have any children?" Cathy asked.

"I had a son, Jacob, but he died," Sam said, sounding as nonplussed as possible.

"Oh my, I'm so sorry," Cathy replied.

"Tell me, did you read the letter my mom wrote me in the back of the journal?" Samantha asked her.

"Yes, yes I did, I read that many times. She said I could. Her words were beautiful, she loved you so much, I can tell you that. She was a beautiful woman and a wonderful friend," Cathy responded.

"Thank you, I would love to hear more about her," Sam said, "and she was right in that letter, painful things in our lives give us wisdom, so I'm much wiser than I would have been without the pain. I envision my mom holding my son, comforting him."

"I'm sure she is with him, her grandbaby, oh that makes me tear up a little. Listen, I will be there, and I look forward to receiving your invitation and seeing your art, but most of all I look forward to seeing you. I haven't seen you since you were so young," Cathy replied.

Chapter 44

Samantha awoke with a start, surprised that she slept in until 9am. Today was her big shopping day with Karen, she remembered, rolling over and covering her head with the pillow as she moaned. Before long, she rolled out of bed, after she decided that she needed to get this day started. Sam suddenly realized that she was to meet Karen at the boutique in less than an hour and took a quick shower. She brushed her hair and put on lipstick and mascara then headed out the door. Karen was already inside the boutique with her sister, even though it wasn't technically opened yet. She let Sam in, and led her to the changing room.

"I took the liberty of picking out some dresses. This is for your art gallery show right?" Karen asked.

"Yes, I'd love something I can wear other times, of course, but I'm getting it for the show," Samantha replied, "and you have no idea how much I appreciate this."

"No worries at all, like I said, I have a gift. I assume that you want something artsy, maybe semi-formal? Anyway, I have 3 picked out and then if you tell me what you like from each I can go from there.

Sam went back to the dressing room and gasped as she saw the dresses. One was an emerald green dress that was cut like a sarong, draping over one shoulder. The second was ice blue with silver embroidery, the top had a boatneck opening and the bottom was a knee length handkerchief skirt. The third one was black with a plunging neckline, and floor length.

"Not the black, I'm sorry, I just wouldn't feel comfortable, not with residents from work there, and a lady who knew me when I was a child. I love the other two though, I will try them on!" Samantha said as she headed into the dressing room. She tried on the green dress first. The fit was impeccable, Sam felt like a princess in this dress. It was understated yet rich. She walked out to the three way mirror to look at herself.

"Wow, Sam, you do make that dress look good," Karen said, grinning as Sam blushed, "look at it from all angles, then go change into that blue beauty, would ya?"

Sam moved around to see all angles, and Karen helped her to position the mirrors around to get a better view. The dress fit perfectly, everywhere. While she moved around to get every view, Karen snapped some pics with her cell phone, "these are for comparison, so you can see both side by side," she told Sam.

Sam changed into the blue dress and gasped. This dress transformed her, from the mousy Samantha that she always imagined she was to a vibrant and beautiful woman. She felt afraid for a moment, afraid of leaving her old self behind if one single other soul saw her in this dress. Taking a deep breath, she bid farewell to that person, and opened the dressing room door.

"Oh my," Karen said, putting her hand to her chest.

"It is as amazing as I think, right?" Sam asked quietly, almost afraid of breaking the spell.

"It is stunning, and I think even that word isn't quite worthy," Karen said.

"This is the one. I can't imagine not wearing this to the opening," Sam said, "in fact, I wish the opening was tonight so I could wear it sooner. I can't believe how easy you made all this. I usually hate shopping, but this was effortless. Lunch is on me, and it still won't feel like I'm doing enough for you. Damn, that means I have to take it off. I'll be back out in a minute."

Sam went into the dressing room and closed the door. She looked at herself in the mirror, still shocked at what she saw. It seemed that she suddenly bloomed and became a woman, an artist, her soul was blossoming. Samantha didn't want to take the dress of, but she did so grudgingly. She lovingly placed the dress back on the hanger and finished getting her clothes on. She carried the dress out as if it were the most valuable treasure ever, and she felt like it was.

"Holy wow, Sam, did something happen in that dressing room?" Karen asked her as she approached her.

"What do you mean?" Sam asked, confused.

"Well, you looked amazing in both dresses, but the blue one... it seemed magical. But even now, after you're back in your clothes, well, it's like you've transformed. I've never seen anything like this," Karen said, circling Samantha as she spoke.

"I do feel different, honestly. I feel like I'm living my life in color, instead of black and white, for the first time ever. So much has changed since I was diagnosed. Sometimes I get upset with myself for not waking up sooner, but then I realize some people never do wake up. I'm so fortunate," Sam said, tears forming in her eyes, "and this dress, it seems to feel so right."

Sam carefully handed the dress to the girl behind the counter as if it could break.

"Would you like to see some accessories to go with this?" the girl asked.

"No, thank you, I think it will be alright on it's own," Sam said. After she paid, the girl got out a garment bag and slipped it over the dress on the hanger. They walked out to Sam's car and she put it in the trunk.

"Would you like to follow me to the cafe or would you like me to drive?" Samantha asked Karen.

"Oh, I walked over here, I live right around the corner, so if I could ride with you, that would be great!" Karen replied.

"I had no idea you lived near here, you are lucky, it's a beautiful area! I will happily drive, I'm excited to share my favorite cafe with you!" Sam said, unlocking the doors.

On her way to the cafe, Sam tilted the visor down to block the sun from her eyes. She had forgotten that she had tucked Zack's card up there for safe keeping, and it fell off, ending up on the edge of her seat.

"I'll get it!" Karen said as she reached for the card, "who is Zack Adams, Esquire?"

"I met him at the gallery the other day, well, in the parking lot. I know very little about him, except he was headed to the gallery so he must like art, and he is gorgeous, and dresses very well," Sam answered, feeling her face heat up a little as she did so.

"Oh really?" Karen replied, "have you been seeing him then?"

"Well, he asked me to call him, but I haven't yet," Sam admitted.

"Why on earth not?" Karen exclaimed, "what about living your life in color?"

"You are right. You are absolutely right, Karen, and thank you for that little shove. I will call him," Sam said.

"No time like the present," Karen said, "how about I get us a table and you come in after you are done?"

"Oh, wow, no pressure, but alright. I will give him a call. I wonder if he remembers me," Sam said, "I will be there in just a few minutes."

Sam watched as Karen walked towards the cafe, and she wondered what she would say to Zack. Knowing that any delays would just make her more nervous, she dialed the phone. After two rings he answered.

"Hello?" he said.

"Hi, this is Samantha, calling for Zack Adams," She replied.

"Oh, Samantha! I was hoping you would call! Your gallery opening is in a few short days, how about that dinner?" Zack said, and Sam could tell he was smiling. She imagined his blue eyes and suddenly was more anxious to see them.

"I would love to! Life is extremely hectic right now, I have a friend coming from out of town, the opening, what if we went to dinner just before the opening? What would you think of that?" Sam asked him.

"I would be honored, m'lady, would it be presumptuous to assume I can accompany you to your opening? I promise to not get in your way," Zack replied.

"I would like that. I have to be at the gallery to address the staff at 4pm, but would be free after that. It will have to be an early dinner, I hope you don't mind," Sam said.

"It sounds perfect, and as a matter of fact, I have to be at the gallery at 4pm that day as well, so we can leave from there if you would like," Zack responded.

"Oh, why will you be at the gallery?" Sam inquired.

"To be addressed by the artist, of course, I'm the owner," Zack said.

"I had no idea," Samantha stammered, "maybe this is a bad idea, I mean, I didn't know you were the owner of the gallery."

"Why would it be a bad idea? Are gallery owners below you? I realize I'm not an artist, but I definitely appreciate the arts, and especially your work," he replied.

"I don't know you well enough to know if you are kidding, but I can assure you I don't think you are below me, quite the opposite. I would love to hear about owning a gallery, and I'm honored that you like my work. I would be glad to go to dinner with you, and to have you accompany me to the show, thank you," Sam said, surprising herself with her self assurance, "I will see you then, Zack."

"I will be looking forward to it, might I suggest either wearing your gallery opening outfit there or bringing it to change into? That way we can have a nice relaxing dinner with no worries about time restriction," he replied.

"That sounds nice, I am looking forward to it. Have a good day," Sam said as she hung up the phone. She rushed into the cafe to Karen.

"Hey, sorry that took so long, are you ready to order?" Samantha said to Karen who had been perusing the menu. They headed up to the counter and each ordered a chicken caesar salad and an iced tea. They took a wooden number for their table and their iced teas and went to sit down.

"Ok, tell me everything," Karen demanded even before they were settled.

"We have a date on my opening day, after I address the staff of the gallery, and before the
show, and I will wear my dress and we will have a leisurely early dinner, oh and he is the gallery owner," Sam said quickly.

"Wait, what?" Karen said, "he is the gallery owner?"

"I was just as surprised as you," Sam assured her, "I had no idea at all. I'm speaking to the staff about my MS at 4pm on the day of the opening, but now I find out that Mr. Gorgeous is going to be there. All of a sudden, I'm so nervous, and somehow I feel so unworthy. I mean, he is a gallery owner!"

At that moment, their food arrived. Two chicken caesar salads, Sam's favorite meal at her favorite cafe.

"You are a soon to be famous artist, there is no way you are unworthy, Sam," Karen said before taking her first bite, "wow, this is delicious!"

They ate in silence for awhile, Karen savoring each bite, and Sam thinking about what Karen had just said, about being a famous artist soon, about a date with Zack, and about talking about her MS in front of the staff, including him. Nothing like starting a date by baring her weaknesses.

"How am I going to talk to the staff about my MS, about my limitations, with him there? Not exactly a romantic start to the relationship, 'hey, date me after I explain how I'm damaged'" Sam said.

"Do you think that he doesn't already know that you have MS? Haven't they interviewed you and put together a brochure about the artist?" Karen asked her, sipping her iced tea.

"You're right. The gallery knows. And he is the gallery owner. So he already knows. I'm not sure what to think about that," Sam said.

"There is nothing to think about, Sam, you said you met him outside the gallery and at that time he didn't know who you were. Yes, you have MS, so what? Here's what I see: you are gorgeous, full of life, full of talent and possibility. You have a spark and your life has just begun. Why wouldn't he want to take you out?" Karen asked.

"Thank you, Karen. You are right, MS does not define me. I need to stop acting like I have a tattoo on my forehead that says I'm dying. I do get that. Time to take a deep breath. This next week is about my art, and I can't believe it's happening. It is all a dream come true, and I'm so hopeful about the future. About my art, about Zack," Sam replied.

"Sam, I'm so glad we are friends. Like I said earlier, this transformation is amazing, and I'm glad I can witness it. I'm looking forward to meeting Zack too," Karen said with a wink, "and I love this cafe! I see why you wanted to come here. This is the best caesar salad that I've ever had!"

"Sometimes I bring my sketchbook or my journal down here, order a yogurt parfait and and iced tea and spend the afternoon, writing, sketching, planning. I love the energy here, it feels so good to me," Sam told her.

"I can see why, it has a great vibe! I love it, and thank you again for everything, unfortunately, I told my neighbor that I would watch her son this afternoon so I need to get back. Could I get a ride?" Karen asked.

"Of course! It's been quite a long day for me, and I'd love to get a bit of a nap in before I clean my apartment," Sam said as they headed to the car.

Chapter 45

Sam took a nap with the knowledge that she was on vacation for ten days. Ten amazing days that would include a visit from someone who knew her mom and an art gallery show, oh and a dream date. She was so glad that she scheduled this time, and that everything in her life was happening exactly as it was. As she drifted off she realized that she never used to nap.

Sam opened her eyes and looked at the clock. 4:05 pm. She stretched her arms over her head and straightened her legs, moaning a bit as she did so. Samantha woke slowly, but almost always felt revived by naps. This one was a bit later in the day, so she likely wouldn't be back in bed until very late, which only meant more cleaning would get done. She sat up and put her legs over the edge of the bed, thinking about all she needed to do. She grabbed her notepad off the nightstand and began her list: mop floors, clean out fridge, make shopping list, sweep, scrub bathroom, file bills away, take out trash/recycling, dust furniture, vacuum, water plants. As a second thought she added 'eat dinner' to the list, since she knew that she would likely forget otherwise. Deciding it was time to get started, she hopped up off the bed.

Sam realized there were things she forgot to add to the list, like laundry and emptying/loading the dishwasher, so she started with those. She loved the thought of the house working while she went on to do other tasks. Cleaning out the fridge didn't take long, as Sam liked to do that on a regular basis. She hated food going to waste so she was constantly going through and using up items in there. After wiping down the interior of the fridge, she gathered up all garbage in the house and tossed it in the bag in the kitchen garbage can. She gathered up the small amount of recycling and carried it all down to the garbage area. As soon as she returned, she scrubbed the bathroom, swept and mopped the bathroom and dining room and started dusting the living room, a task that took a very small effort, then vacuumed.

Samantha decided to rest a bit before emptying the dishwasher and moving the laundry over. She picked up her mom's journal and got cozy on the couch. This time she turned to the beginning of the book. Her mom started journaling when she was diagnosed with MS. Sam was four, and Barbara was devastated to receive the news. The treatments at the time were extremely limited, and it was, in fact, a death sentence. Barbara was distraught and wanted to make sure that she lived out her life with someone who would care for Samantha, so she moved back home to her parent's house.

Barbara struggled with that decision, both for the fairness to Samantha, and the fairness to her own parents who were preparing to retire and travel. She was weakening though, her MS was getting worse, so Barbara had no other options. She knew that Samantha was loved, and they would do their best to raise her. Barbara also knew she would be taken care of and could watch her daughter grow up as long as she was alive.

Sam felt the tears flow down her cheek while she read a passage about her mom visiting with Cathy's husband, Mike in the back yard. "I talk to Mike sometimes for hours on end, he is an old soul, I can tell. We talk about dreams for our children, about the dreams we had for ourselves, what we have to let go of, what we can hold on to. I told him that I'd give my life for Sam's future, and in the next breath I told him I would dance with him after a cure was found for this wretched disease. I have to hold out hope that I am part of Samantha's future. I can't leave that little girl without a mother."

Sam closed the journal and wiped her tears. She had never really thought about her mother's love for her before. She found herself both sad and comforted by reading the journal. Small doses, though. Sam knew that once she was done reading it, that it wouldn't be new to her any longer. For now she put it away. She walked into the kitchen to empty the dishwasher. Sam noticed as she was putting the dishes away that she was seeing things differently. Look how far she had come, from that little girl with a sick mother. She knew her mother would be proud of her. The phone rang, startling Samantha.

"Hello?" she said into her cell.

"Samantha? This is Cathy. I just want you to know I will be on the road first thing in the morning, so there by early afternoon, okay?" Cathy said to her.

"I'm so looking forward to it, Cathy. You have my address, and if you have any issues finding me, just call," Sam responded.

"Oh honey, I've been so excited, I've programmed you into my GPS and I've mapped it out! I'm bringing a fancy dress for your art show, and I've found some more pictures of your family that I'm going to bring. I can't wait to see you!" Cathy said.

"I can't wait either!" Sam replied, "I will have lunch ready for you, ok?"

"Sounds wonderful! I will see you then!" Cathy said as she hung up.

Sam looked at her watch and realized why her stomach was growling. She went through the cabinets, starting a list of things to buy at the store in the morning, but for tonight decided on a peanut butter and jelly sandwich. She ate quietly at the table and tried to remember the last time she had a pb&j. Maybe sometime last year. She often added peanut butter into her smoothies for some protein, and had toast with jelly, but a good old fashioned peanut butter and jelly sandwich had not been enjoyed by her in a long time. She savored every bite and drank a tall glass of milk as well. She put her dishes in the dishwasher as soon as she was done and went to finish the laundry. Just as she put the last shirt away she realized it was getting late.

She grabbed up her cell phone, a clean towel and a book then headed for the bath. She filled the tub with water that was just under what she would consider 'hot' and eased her way in. Her cell was on the edge of the tub and she began reading her book. Sam loved her baths, she always had. She wondered briefly if her mom had been like her. Did she like peanut butter and jelly sandwiches? Did she enjoy baths? She could ask Cathy some of her questions, and the journal may answer some as well. A wave of gratitude washed over her. Everything in her life felt like a miracle. Sam took a deep breath and opened her book to read as she soaked. Samantha had lost herself in books since she was a kid. She remembered Cathy would be outside in a lawn chair tanning and reading a book. Sometimes Samantha would go sit in a chair next to her and read her book. They wouldn't speak for hours, the only sound would be the flipping of pages.

Sam read until she noticed the water cooling off. That was always her cue that the bath was over and the story must wait until another day. Oh, some days she drained a bit of water and ran some more hot water in, but tonight she was tired. She drained the tub and dried off, glad she didn't get her hair wet this close to bed time. She put her book on her nightstand, pulled up the covers and turned off the light. Some nights she tossed and turned, but tonight she was out within seconds.

Chapter 46

The sunshine coming through the window eased Sam awake. She stretched and thought about her day before getting up. Samantha mentally made a list. She would shower, get dressed, have some cereal, then go to the grocery store and come put it away. Then she would try to rest a bit before making lunch for Cathy because she wanted to have energy while she was here. Samantha was glad that Cathy came early and they would have today and all day tomorrow to visit before her show.

Sam looked through the grocery ads in the newspaper as she ate her cereal. She circled things she needed that were on sale and cut a couple coupons prior to leaving the house. Sam had decided on a tossed green salad with grilled chicken for lunch, so she bought several different kinds of dressings, some croutons, and cheeses. She didn't know if Cathy would want to eat out or stay in for the other meals, but bought plenty of options just in case every meal would be prepared by her. Once she was done at the store, and all the groceries were put away, Sam was drained. She laid on the couch for a half hour, knowing that would be enough to refresh her. After her nap she cooked the chicken and prepped the salad, then sat down to read her book as she waited for Cathy's arrival.

Sam was so engrossed in the book that she didn't hear Cathy's car outside. She jumped as she heard the knock on the door. Sam tripped on the coffee table, slamming her knee into the floor on the way to answer it.

"Ouch, damnit" she whispered, then yelled "I'm coming!" towards the door. "Hi there! Sorry it took so long, I'm clumsy these days," Sam said as she opened the door. Cathy was standing there, already teary-eyed, waiting for Samantha to open the door and just as she did so, Cathy moved forward to hug her.

"It's been too long, way too long," she said to Sam, then, pulling back, "let me look at you. Wow. You look exactly like your mom. It's remarkable."

"Come on in, I'm so glad you are here," Sam said, feeling a little nervous.

"Oh, I'm glad I'm here too. Thrilled to see you. And now, to see how much like Barbara you look, you are her spitting image, I just can't get over it," Cathy gushed.

"Are you hungry? I have everything prepared, just need to throw it together whenever you are ready," Sam said.

"Actually, yes, I'm starving. Thank you so much. I would love to take you out for dinner tonight if you are free, and how can I help you to get lunch together?" Cathy replied.

"I thought we would have a green salad with grilled chicken, so if you'd like to get the plates out, I'll get everything out and we can just plate it up," Sam said, pointing to the cabinet where the plates are.

They worked side by side, plating the salads, as if they had been doing this for a lifetime. Sam was impressed by how easy it all was. Cathy seemed to know her way around Sam's kitchen already.

"Iced tea?" Sam asked.

"Yes, please," Cathy replied, "I'm going to go ahead and take the plates to the table."

As they ate, Cathy told Sam stories of her mom, many Sam had already read in the journal but it was amazing to hear Cathy tell them. Cathy also told stories of her children, and now grandchildren. She also talked about Sam's grandparents who she respected deeply. Sam was thankful that Cathy was occupying the conversation, she didn't really know what to say, but also she was thoroughly enjoying hearing all of the stories.

They spent the entire afternoon talking about Barbara, about her hopes and dreams for Sam, about the heartbreak of her illness, and then about Sam's life, her hopes and dreams. Sam told Cathy how she had been closed off and cold, about how Jacob's death affected her, about how she cried during her pregnancy because she wanted her mom there. She also told her a little bit about her breakdown and about how painting saved her.

"Would you like a sneak peek at the art show?" Sam asked Cathy.

"Oh my, I would love that!" Cathy squealed.

"I've made arrangements to stop by there before dinner. I need to do my final check before the show. It shouldn't take long, but you can stay as long as you'd like," Sam told her.

"I just can't believe I know a famous artist. Your mother would be so proud of you. I know I am sounding like a broken record, but I just know she would be thrilled at the thought of a gallery show that's all yours. You must be quite an artist to have your own show," Cathy said.

"Do we need to get you checked into your hotel? Would you like a little bit to get settled before we go?" Sam asked her, blushing.

"Oh yes, I do need to check in, and maybe put my bags in there, but besides that, I'm ready to go wherever you would like to go," Cathy replied.

Sam followed her to her hotel and after Cathy got her bags in her room, Sam drove her to the gallery. She was thrilled to be taking her for her own private gallery show. Sure, Sam had to check the labeling and pricing, but Cathy would get to see all the art, and spend as long as she would like alone with it.

At the gallery, Sam was thrilled to see that everything looked perfect, and she was kind of in shock about the pricing. She felt like Patricia knew what she was doing though, so she didn't worry. She watched as Cathy walked painting to painting, gasping often, wiping tears. Sam watched her make her way around the room, realizing this was her connection to her mom. Suddenly, she found herself wiping tears, and when she looked up from doing so, she saw Zack.

"Um, hi. How are you?" she said to him.

"It's great seeing you, but are you ok?" Zack replied.

"I'm perfectly fine, thanks! See that lady over there?" Sam said, pointing towards Cathy, "she was friends with my mom, so this is kind of like my mom seeing my work."

Zack sat down next to her, "well that must be fantastic, then. I was worried that something was wrong. Glad to hear that's not the case. Are you ready for your show?"

"I am. Perhaps not ready to talk to the staff prior to the show, but I'm ready for my show," Sam admitted to him.

"Why are you concerned about meeting with the staff?" Zack asked.

"Honestly? I'm mostly worried about you hearing about my limitations," Sam admitted.

"Sam, I read the flyer Gina put together, and even more, I was in on the vote to get your show in the gallery. I know you have MS, I've even done some research as to what that means. I'm looking forward to getting to know you and all that entails. I'm fascinated by you, by your creativity, and yes, by your story. The fact that you have MS is not a dealbreaker with me. I didn't set out to be attracted to you, when Gina presented your art, your story, I was intrigued, but when I met you, I was struck by your beauty, your energy, and then when I found out who you were, I tied it together with your art and well, I was smitten.

Don't let my presence hold you back from telling all of us what you need at your show," Zack replied.

Sam didn't know how to respond. She opened her mouth to speak, but then closed it. Finally, after a pause, she looked into his eyes and said "thank you."

Those eyes, Samantha felt like she may melt into them. She was thankful when she heard Cathy walking up. Clearing her throat, she found the ability to speak again.

"Cathy, this is Zack. He is the gallery owner. Zack, Cathy has known me since I was a young girl and she traveled to see my show," Sam said, standing to face both of them at once.

"It's nice to meet you, Zack," Cathy said, extending her hand.

"It's wonderful meeting you," he said, shaking her hand, "what do you think of Samantha's work?"

"I love it so much, I'm just in awe of the paintings, and of her," Cathy said.

"I know exactly what you mean," Zack said, looking at Sam, "I will leave you two alone. Sam, 4 o'clock tomorrow?"

"I will be there," Sam said, with a smile.

Samantha and Cathy both watched him walk away.

"He's a good looking man," Cathy said, winking at Sam.

"Yes, he is, did you have any questions about any of the paintings?" Sam asked, changing the subject. They walked from painting to painting and Cathy asked questions about what each symbolized, what she was feeling when she painted it, if each was painted with anyone in mind, etc.

"Oh dear, I've taken up a lot of your time," Cathy said, noticing that over two hours had passed since Sam asked her if she had questions about the paintings.

"There's nothing I would rather have been doing tonight, Cathy, I'm so thankful you came into town for my show, and I'm even more thankful for the box you had mailed me," Sam said.

"It's the least I could do, dear," Cathy said, giving her a small hug, "and I'm really hungry, how about you?"

"Famished actually, where would you like to go?" Sam asked her.

"Do you know of any good pubs? I just love pub food," Cathy responded.

Sam took her to the pub that she and John used to frequent, and they sat in a booth against the back wall. The waitress brought menus and a bowl of peanuts in the shell. Cathy looked at Sam quizzically when Samantha shelled her peanuts and tossed the shells on the floor. It actually took the waitress telling Cathy that it was alright for Cathy to follow suit, but soon they were both tossing peanut shells and giggling. Sam looked up when the waitress was bringing their food and saw John walk in. She didn't know how to respond, she had not seen him since the yard sale. She wasn't sure if she should hide, look away, wave, or approach him. Before she could think about it too much, he saw her and was headed her way.

"Hey Sam!" John said, bending down to kiss her on the cheek, "you look great! How have you been?"

"I've been great, John, it's good to see you! This is my friend, Cathy, actually, she lived next door to me when I was young and was friends with my mom. Cathy, this is my ex husband, John," Sam said, introducing them.

"Oh wow, it's great to meet you, Cathy," John said, smiling at her, "Sam, it's great to see you, I am meeting up with some guys from work, so I need to go, but it was nice running into you."

"You too, John, take care," Sam said, feeling a little sad to see him walk away.

Cathy watched Sam's expressions as she took a bite of her burger, "are you alright, sweetie?" she asked Samantha.

"Yeah, I'm alright. John is a good man and was an excellent husband. I just couldn't let him be my excellent husband, you know?" Sam asked, wiping a tear away.

"Yes dear, I know, trust me," Cathy said, patting Sam's hand.

Chapter 47

The ringing phone woke Sam the next morning, "hello?" she said, groggily.

"Oh, I didn't mean to wake you. I'm glad I called before coming over, though. Will you give me a call back when you are awake?" Cathy said.

"Cathy! I am getting up right now. Why don't you head over? I'm just going to hop into the shower but I will leave the door unlocked. Make yourself at home and I will make us some breakfast," she responded.

"That sounds great, I will be over in a few, dear," Cathy said before hanging up.

Sam jumped up out of bed and started feeling a little nauseated when she realized today was the big day. She was thankful Cathy was in town and would be around today, so she wouldn't just be waiting all day. Sam unlocked the door then got in the shower. She thought about the things she would say to the gallery staff today. She wondered who would be at the show, and she pondered where Zack would be taking her. Sam knew that tonight would require a bit of extra rest, and thought that maybe she and Cathy could stay in, order a pizza when it was lunch time and she hoped to get a short nap.

"Cathy? Are you here?" Sam yelled when she got out of the shower.

"I'm here, but do whatever you need to do, dear, would you like me to start some breakfast?" Cathy responded.

"Oh sure, that would be great. I have everything for biscuits and sausage gravy; breakfast burritos; bacon, eggs and toast... Just look around, and start whatever sounds good to you. I will be out shortly," Sam said before closing her door to get dressed. Sam put on a tank top and yoga pants and combed her hair.

"That bacon smells amazing, Cathy. Thank you for starting it. Did you sleep alright?" Sam said as she walked out of her room.

"Oh yes, I slept beautifully! Today is your big day! I've found everything I need, I will make breakfast, you just relax. In fact, anything that needs done today, you just let me know, alright?" Cathy said, looking at Samantha sternly.

"Well, I do appreciate that. I figured we could just have pizza delivered for lunch. Then I have to go to the gallery at 4 to talk to the staff, and well, Zack and I have a date between that and the time the show opens at 7. I hate to leave you alone for dinner..." Sam began, but was interrupted by Cathy.

"Nonsense! Don't think twice about me and dinner. I'm a big girl and I saw a cafe right next to the hotel that I'd like to try. Plus, at my age it takes a little time to get all done up for a fancy event like an art show. Actually, I don't think I've ever been to an art show in my life, imagine that! This whole trip has been one for the record books, I can assure you! I do hope we keep in touch after all this," she said.

"We will make sure of it!" Sam replied, "I'm so excited about tonight, but so nervous too. I can't remember the last time I felt this nervous. Of course, when you add in a first date with Zack, I just want to crawl under a rock."

"Everything will be perfect, I'm sure of it. I know that your mom used to tire easily. Will you need a nap today?" Cathy asked as she sat Sam's plate in front of her.

"Yes, I'm hoping to lay down for a little bit, but I'm also not planning on tiring myself out too much today. I can't wait for you to see my dress, but I think it looks much better on, so I guess you'll see it tonight," she said laughing.

"Alright, a bit after lunch I will head out, I know I'd like to get a nap today too. It's going to be a big night for my friend Barbara's daughter. I know she's smiling down on you," Cathy said to her, then they both began to eat in silence.

The rest of the day felt very lazy to Sam, but that's exactly what she had been hoping for. Just as scheduled, a bit after lunch (they opted for a light lunch of soup and salad instead of pizza), Cathy went to her hotel and Sam took a nap. She slept for over an hour before waking and starting to get ready for the evening. Samantha was thankful that she didn't sleep longer because she loved to take her time with hair and makeup before going out. She didn't like to feel rushed, so this felt perfect.

Sam straightened her hair, opting to leave it down for the evening. She chose understated makeup, but opted for dramatic eyes and a red tint on her lips. At 3:40 pm, Sam was walking out the door, feeling like a princess. Her small silver handbag went beautifully with the dress, and she was thrilled about that since she had forgotten to check before today. She didn't have a lot to say to the staff at the gallery, but did have some things she needed, like places to sit periodically and wanted them to know signs that she was in trouble or overly fatigued.

Sam had been doubling up her physical therapy for weeks to help ensure her footdrop wouldn't be an issue and she wore flats to keep her stable. In her handbag, in addition to lipstick and her cell phone, she had a granola bar just in case. Sam felt quite prepared for the evening.

She made it through addressing the staff. Gina had already had them place chairs throughout, and many of them told her they had done a little bit of research on their own. Zack seemed to be riveted to her the whole time, holding back, not crowding her while she spoke, but hanging on her every word. When she was done speaking, the staff began approaching her and shaking her hand, many told her that she could count on them, others complimented her work. Sam was a bit overwhelmed by the time Zack made his way to her.

"Shall we get out of here?" he asked, extending his arm to her. She put her hand in the crook of his elbow and smiled.

"Absolutely, thank you," Sam replied.

She noticed once they got in the car that it was five o'clock. Two hours before her show, two hours to spend with Zack. So far, she realized, he was easy to be around. He hadn't asked where she wanted to go, nor had he asked what types of food she liked. A classical cd was playing softly in the car, and she relaxed into the seat and looked sideways to admire him. Zack was gorgeous, his jaw was finely chiseled, his eyes... oh, his eyes. He smiled as he felt her eyes on him.

"Are you ready to be famous, mon cherie?" he asked.

"Not sure about being famous, and I'm not even sure I'm totally ready for tonight, but I'm as ready as I'm going to be," she said, "I'm pretty nervous. Though, I've been nervous every step of the way and so far there has been absolutely nothing to be worried about."

"You have nothing to worry about with me, I promise," he said as he reached over to caress her hand. Electricity shot through her and she was thankful she was sitting down. Suddenly, Sam felt so alive, and she imagined leaning over and kissing Zack. She quickly changed her focus to try to figure out where he was taking her. She didn't recognize the area, but then saw a sign of a famous French restaurant. She had heard Connie talking about going there many years ago, but had never been. Sam couldn't believe this is where Zack was taking her.

"We have arrived, mon cherie," Zack said as he handed his keys to the valet. Before she knew it, he was opening her door.

"Thank you, Zack, thank you for this," Sam began.

"The pleasure is all mine, I assure you. My hope is that this is one night of many," Zack replied.

Throughout dinner they discussed their lives, Zack seemed to have an idyllic childhood but had recently lost his father. Samantha reached over to touch his hand as he talked about what a great man his dad was. She felt the electricity again but did not pull away. Instead, she looked into his eyes and melted into them. He leaned forward, kissing her lightly on the lips. They were interrupted by the waiter who was bringing the wine.

"Only a sip for me," Samantha said, waving off the waiter when he paused.

"Yes, it's a big night, just a sip for now. Samantha, have I told you how beautiful you are tonight?" Zack said, reaching again for her hand.

"Thank you," Samantha replied, blushing.

Sam found herself telling him about her first marriage, about Jacob, about how she was cold and unfeeling. She couldn't believe how easy Zack was to talk to. They ate while they talked, pausing only as plates were being put down in front of them or being taken away.

"Oh, it's time for me to get my Cinderella to her ball," Zack said, placing his napkin on the table and standing up. Before she could respond, he was behind her chair, ready to help her up. Samantha was not used to such chivalry. As they walked out, he had his hand on the small of her back and she felt the electricity again. His car was waiting for them near the door and the valet had her door open for her. When she approached the door, he leaned forward and kissed her deeply, embracing her. She relaxed into him, feeling his energy surge through her. Abruptly he pulled away, and shut her door as soon as she was seated. As he got in the car, she looked at him quizzically, wondering why he stopped so abruptly.

"You are beautiful, and I'm so attracted to you, deeply attracted. If I hadn't stopped myself you would never get to your show on time," Zack explained and looked at her. He smiled as he saw her close her eyes and smile, resting her head against the back of her seat.

When she opened them, they were arriving at the gallery. Sam could not believe how packed the parking lot was already. He took note as she inhaled deeply.

Chapter 48

"This is your night. Everything will go beautifully," Zack said, kissing her on the cheek, "why don't you head in and I will be around. This is your night, mon cherie."

Sam took a deep breath and walked inside. All talking stopped when she stepped into the room, and some even applauded. She felt like the room was starting to spin, and Gina was quickly at her side, balancing her, leading her in. Sam looked around and saw Connie, Ellen, Jack and his wife, Bill's family, Karen, Cathy, and just as she turned around, she saw John walk in. Gina handed her a champagne flute and guided her to a painting.

"Don't worry dear, it's sparkling water. I wanted to give you something to do, you look a little unsteady, I met your friend Cathy and she is going to come over and enquire about this painting. Use the time to breathe and then move on to your public, just go as slow as you'd like," Gina instructed. Before Sam could thank her, Cathy was at her side and Gina was walking across the room towards her mother. The crowd seemed to be looking at the art and talking amongst themselves. Cathy started telling her everything about the painting, Sam laughed as she realized that Cathy was parroting her from the day before.

"I'm so glad you are here, Cathy. It means the world to me," Sam said, hugging her.

"It's my pleasure. Anytime you are ready or think you need to go talk to others, feel free. This is such an amazing night, and I think it's the beginning of a profitable art career for you. It seems that many of your paintings have a sold sticker on the label already," Cathy told her.

Sam gasped, "really?"

Cathy simply nodded, "there is a couple approaching you, don't worry about me."

Sam turned to see Jack and his wife walking up to her, "Thank you for being here, Jack! So nice to see you, Angie. Thank you for coming."

"The pleasure is ours, Samantha. How lovely to be friends with a famous artist!" Angie responded.

By the end of the evening, Sam had spoken with everyone. That is, everyone but John, as she looked around, Samantha didn't see him anywhere. She had an exhilarating night and she was exhausted. Suddenly, she saw Zack walking towards her. Sam knew he had been there all night, she felt his presence, he calmed her.

"I'd like to offer you a ride home, mon cherie," Zack said as he approached.

"Oh, but I brought my car," Sam replied.

"I can have your car brought to you tomorrow if you'd like. I know you've had a long day," he said.

Sam agreed, but wouldn't go until the last guest had gone. He held her hand all the way to her apartment, caressing it as he drove.

"Samantha, I would love to see you again. I know that we just met but it feels like you are part of my soul already. I don't want to scare you away, but I can't imagine my life without you. It's almost like I didn't know it before, but now I realize I've been living my life in black and white and you have brought color in it."

That was all he had to say.

www.ingramcontent.com/pod-product-compliance
Lightning Source LLC
Chambersburg PA
CBHW051436170626
46809CB00006B/2488